MARIO PUZO

INSIDE LAS VEGAS

NEIL
DIAMOND
DELTA-NATIONAL-UNITED-WESTERN

Color photography by JOHN LAUNOIS

Black-and-white photography by MICHAEL ABRAMSON and SUSAN FOWLER-GALLAGHER

MARIO PUZO

INSIDE LAS VEGAS

GROSSET & DUNLAP
A FILMWAYS COMPANY
PUBLISHERS · NEW YORK

To Virginia Cornacchia Puzo

Published simultaneously in Canada
Library of Congress catalog card number: 77-71303
ISBN 0-448-12462-9
First printing 1977
Printed in the United States of America
An excerpt from *Mario Puzo Inside Las Vegas* originally appeared in *Playboy* magazine

DESIGNED BY ROBERT S. NEMSER

WAYNE
NEWTON

LAS VEGAS
24 hour entertainment

CONTENTS

Introduction

Sore losers have always given gambling a bad name. Down through the ages.

Obnoxious winners haven't helped. Offensively they claim their success comes through God's love, then spend their holy lucky winnings on booze, whores, and more gambling.

Then there are moralizing kibitzers: social reformers, religious leaders, political economists and theorists, even philosophers and psychiatrists. Almost universally they condemn gambling.

And there are the natural hazards of gambling. The readers of marked cards, the riggers of loaded dice, the Satanic fixers of sacred sports events.

Given all this, it is amazing that the gambling lust still rages in the heart of man. But the truth is that gambling is a primitive religious instinct peculiar to our species.

Cunningly modern man indulges a primitive idolatry, masked as a degenerate beguilement, with the graven images of roulette wheels, gaily colored, ritualistically sequenced playing cards, and plastic cubed dice that eons ago were made from the bones of dinosaurs and antelopes.

More than other basically human appetites, gambling has been condemned as a vice without a redeeming virtue or a pardonable excuse. Drunkards are tragic or romantic, murderers interesting, gourmands and sex aficionados are approved of as at least getting something for their money. Politicians

NEVADA
5-77
LOVEYA

and businessmen, most of them deadly enemies of the human spirit, are applauded as servers and builders of our society. Religious leaders, those supreme hustlers of the long shot, are revered. But gamblers are sneered at because most people think of gambling as a FOOLISH vice. You give away your money for nothing.

Then why do I believe that gambling has bettered my character, kept me out of prison, helped me to bring up five children pleasurably and, I think, more or less successfully? Well, gambling has helped preserve my marriage for thirty years by keeping me too busy to chase other women and too guilty to resent my wife and children for having to support them, has forced me to write more by putting me into debt, and has improved my health by forcing me to learn how to play tennis at gambling resorts in order to stay out of casinos.

This is a book about Las Vegas. But I was chosen to do it, I think, because I have the reputation of being a degenerate gambler. So there is no way for me to write about Vegas without being a little personal. And there is also no way to write about the amazing birth and growth of Vegas without writing about gambling as it existed since the beginning of recorded history, the larceny it has seeded in the human heart, the tragedies in the countless millions. But in the literature I have read, what's left out are the solace and pleasure it brought countless millions living in worlds without hope and without those dreams essential to life.

This is not a justification of gambling. It is not a glorification of Las Vegas and its gambling culture. But it is certainly not a moral or social condemnation of them. It is merely a recognition that gambling is one of the primary drives of mankind. As such it does a lot of harm—as do wars, industrial inventions, organized religions, and sex. But so what? Maybe we would be better off without gambling but such a thought is completely irrelevant. You can't ever get rid of gambling and the best place to lose your money is Las Vegas. (The nicest place to win is the South of France.)

But to be half-assed honest this book will also try to explain why people love to gamble. Why it makes life bearable for so many people and why even though you wind up a "loser" in the long run, the short run "wins" can make it worthwhile for all but the degenerate gambler.

Las Vegas itself is the big bet won, the miracle happening. An act of faith, possibly by the devil. There is no reason for Las Vegas to exist out there alone in the vast desert of Nevada. But its billions of watts of neon light a Mecca for countless people from all corners of the globe. They come to Vegas to gamble and pray for miracles.

This book won't help them.

WILDERNESS AND NEON

The sailing of the Mayflower to colonize the New World was financed by a lottery in England. So much for our Puritan heritage.

One of the Twelve Apostles was chosen by lot or lottery. But it wasn't Judas.

George Washington never told a lie but he gambled on anything, anyplace, anytime. The night he crossed the Delaware to surprise the Hessians may have been the one night he didn't play cards or shoot craps during the Revolutionary War. (But he knew gambling was bad because he published army orders forbidding enlisted men to gamble.)

Yale, Harvard, and Dartmouth were built with funds raised by lottery. So were many of the first Puritan churches in the New World and the first schools and bridges. Lotteries supplied funds to pay the Revolutionary Army and win our independence.

These facts are cited merely to show that gambling is not an unnatural vice and that the city of Las Vegas is not the invention of the devil and un-American. Nothing can be done about the feeling that Vegas is an uncouth, money-grubbing, sex- and sin-laden metropolis, vulgar in its architecture and its culture. Nothing can be done because it's too hard to disprove. This is just a book about Vegas as a dream world of pleasure, supplying one of the basic needs of human nature.

But still there is a time and place for everything. There is a time for champagne and there is a time for Coca-Cola. There is a time for French haute cuisine and a time for pizza. There is a time for James Joyce and a time for Agatha Christie. There is a time for lust and a time for true love. There is a time for a two-week celibate retreat to a monastery and there is a time for three days of gambling, boozing, and wild women in Vegas. So a book about Las Vegas can't hurt. And who knows, wisdom can be acquired by indulging a vice as well as protecting a virtue. Maybe a little something can be learned.

But just to save time, here are a few hard facts. I love Las Vegas but I must tell you that you cannot wind up a winner there over any period of time. It's just that the house percentage or "Edge" cannot be beat by an honest player. Not because casinos are dishonest. They are the first honest gaming establishments in the history of civilization, and gambling has existed since the recorded history of man.

So this book will not tell you how to win. There is no way. It will tell you how not to get killed and that is very simple. Never sign a *marker* or IOU. Never make out a check. Just gamble with the money you bring there.

Sure, you may win on some trips. You may win five, six, or seven trips in a row. But eventually you will get wiped

GOLDEN GATE
ASINO
HOTEL
SINO
PAID
EVERY 15

out. Remember, a losing streak is far more deadly than a winning streak is benevolent. And that's all you have to know about gambling in Vegas. Later on there will be some instruction on percentage gambling. Good luck.

Remember that thirty years ago Las Vegas was a small town with a few Western-style casinos you could break with a fifty-grand win. It is now a city with a billion-dollar gambling plant of luxury hotels that generates close to two billion dollars in WINNINGS A YEAR. *Remember always:* The money to build that billion-dollar gambling plant came from LOSERS.

Now that this basic truth is mentioned, something else can also be said. On a three-day visit to Vegas you can have one of the best times of your life. To do that you have to forget about great museums, the pleasure of reading, great theater, great music, stimulating lectures by great philosophers, great food, great wine, and true love. Forget about them. Just for three days. Believe me, you won't miss them. Ye shall be as little children again.

Today Las Vegas is perhaps the best-known city in the entire world. A newspaper story datelined Las Vegas will immediately get space in any newspaper on the globe. Travel through the centers of civilization in Europe and ask any taxi driver or hotel waiter a question about Las Vegas and you will have his immediate attention. Go East to Japan and Hong Kong and the people there will talk to you about

Downtown Las Vegas—where all the bargains are.

FLAMINGO SHOWROOM
HOORAY 76
A BI-CENSATIONAL REVUE!
COCKTAIL SHOWS $9.76 PER PERSON
8 PM & MIDNIGHT
TIBOR RUDAS PRODUCTION
TROPHY LOUNGE - 7PM TO 5AM
THE SMITH BROTHERS
LAVELLE
LAURA
RICH BONO DUO
THE SPEAKEASY
SPECIAL 14 OZ. T-BONE DINNER
THE PRIME RIB ROOM
COMPLETE DINNER
NEW! BICENTENNIAL BUFFETS
LUNCHEON $2.45 / DINNER $2.90
SERVED IN THE MOJAVE ROOM
CASINO
TEXACO
CIGARETTES
HOT DOGS
LIQUOR

PLAY QUARTERS • WIN CARS & GASOLIN
PLAY QUARTERS WIN CARS GAS
PLAY QUARTERS WIN CARS & GAS

Las Vegas and how they hope one day to go there. Not to make their fortune. They just want to see it.

And the irony is that there is no reason for the existence of Las Vegas except that it has legalized gambling. It is a desert in the middle of nowhere. It has no virtues of climate or natural resources. It has no ancient history or scenery to beguile the tourist. By all rights it should be still a dusty little town with a honky-tonk bust-out gambling joint and a few grubby motels. It should be a railroad whistle-stop instead of a small metropolis which receives thousands of jet planes each year. How did such a miracle happen? Well, to be quite honest and frank about it, Las Vegas is the product of men reputed to have the most cunning criminal minds that America or the world has ever produced. And it is no small tribute to the dazzling alchemy of American democratic capitalism that the whole operation has turned out to be one of the most creditable achievements of our society. Decadent society though it may be.

There may be some who feel that Vegas is an abomination and should be destroyed. They would then have to argue, with me at least, that the oil companies are straight, the stock market is not a flimflam, and that our South American foreign policy is not insane. They would even have to argue that the Democratic Party and the Republican Party are more honest than the Mafia.

And more bargains.

30 GIRLS
AVAILABLE
TO PLEASE
2303
SWINGING
ESCORTS
It's LEGAL
IN
NEVADA
Call 732

Gambling has been a very important part of my life, and not a completely destructive part. Las Vegas was my Mecca and I finally got there in 1964. This may seem to be too personal a remark for a book about Las Vegas but there is no other way to write about gambling. It may also seem to indicate a shallowness of character. And this is partly true. I also have to admit that gambling has been terribly destructive to certain periods of my life. My second novel took ten years to write, partly because I spent too much time gambling and partly because I spent too much time supporting my family. And yet gambling, though it sometimes saved me from despair, has never led me to despair. The reason for this is that I never had that much to lose, and when I did, I finally curtailed my gambling. I believe it to be true that gambling has destroyed the lives of many. But so have booze, women, true love, patriotism, art, the law in all its majesty, and religion.

Las Vegas opulence is available to anyone regardless of race, class, appearance, religion, etc. All you need is a small bankroll. And then you get a taste of the luxuriousness of kings, beautiful women befitting a sultan's harem, spectacular shows with great popular artists of song and dance and mime.

The one thing you won't get is art. But in its place plenty of religion. Vegas boasts more churches per capita than any city in the world.

It doesn't matter that the food is never of haute cuisine quality nor is the service top-notch. Nor does it matter that many of the spectacular glittering shows only rarely have an ounce of real beauty or wit. It is all a dream. It has nothing to do with reality. It is a sanctuary from the real world, real troubles, real emotion, and it's somehow fitting and proper that the city of Las Vegas is surrounded by a vast desert. A desert which acts as a *cordon sanitaire.*

I have always loved Vegas but though I once established a residence there I have rarely been able to stay more than three or four days. I also would not vote for casino gambling to be legalized generally throughout the nation. This is, remember, not the belief of a hidebound Puritan but that of a man who loves gambling and has indulged in it all his life. Maybe I like the idea that I have to travel to get to a gaming city. I know I'd be scared to death to live in a city that has twenty-four hour gambling.

For Vegas is unique in its gambling twenty-four hours a day. Everything is oriented to gambling. There is very little else to do. In the summer it is too hot to play tennis outdoors, in the winter it is too windy. They play a lot of golf there, and nearly everybody bets on the games and there may be as many sucker bets on the course as there are in the casinos. There is not much sightseeing. You can go see Hoover Dam and that's it. You can do a little boating on Lake Mead. There's horseback riding. And of course you can lie by the pool. Which is never more than a two-minute walk from the casino.

In the Bahamas the casinos do not open until one in the afternoon or eight in the evening. In Puerto Rico it is eight in the evening. And in those places the climate is great and the beaches and oceans beautiful. So by the time you play some tennis, swim in the warm blue seas, have a late dinner, it is 11 P.M. The casinos close at 4 A.M. That gives them only five hours to grind you out with their percentages. In that short time you can get hurt but with just a little bit of discretion there is no way to get killed. In twenty-four-hour nonstop Vegas you can get killed betting dollar chips.

But if you like to gamble, really like to gamble, Vegas is the essence. In Europe gambling is at such a slow refined pace that it becomes something else. There is no nervous tension, the gambling tension of a Vegas crap table that sends adrenalin racing through your body. In Vegas you get at least five spins of the roulette wheel to one spin in Cannes. Baccarat flows at the same ratio.

It can be argued that the Vegas kind of excitement is a degeneracy. But still this urge to gamble has enthralled mankind through recorded time, and so must fill some kind of human need. At any rate, it is too late to get rid of Vegas. At one time there was a danger that the citizens of Nevada would vote it into oblivion. Now that gambling employs 28 percent of the work force that danger has vanished. There was a time not too long ago when the federal government and the Congress considered banning gambling casinos because of links to the underworld. Robert Kennedy had his bad eye on Vegas. But if gambling were federally banned, over a billion dollars in Vegas capital investment and income would be wiped out and that is not possible in a democratic capitalistic society. Look at cigarettes.

My introduction to casino gambling was as romantic as any novelist could wish. In 1939 I was sent to Civilian Conservation Corps camp in Lovelock, Nevada. Outside the town and our camp were two whorehouses called "My Place" and "Jo Ann's." (How come I remember those names after nearly forty years?) In the town movie houses whenever a film character said "Let's go over to my place," the whole theater would give a cheer. But Lovelock was only a couple of hours from Reno which was then *the* gambling city.

One day in 1939, as a teenager from New York, I sat in a casino in Reno decorated like Hell, rock-red walls, hostesses wearing devils' tails, mascaraed eyes under devil-horned caps. Sinful, Sinful, Sinful. I spent my

last three dollars buying sucker drinks for a pretty hostess, not even knowing that for an extra two dollars she would have gone to bed. She was so beautiful that it never even occurred to me that she was a hooker. That night I slept a few hours on wooden tables in the back room provided especially for bust-out gamblers. But now I realize I was never a degenerate gambler. A degenerate gambler would never spend his last three dollars buying drinks for a pretty girl. He would have tried to get lucky at craps.

Since I had foolishly lost my entire $23 bankroll and couldn't get back to camp, I went down to the railroad and kindly men put me on a locomotive going to Lovelock to pick up some freight cars. I rode beside the engineer and will never forget that ride through the desert with dawn breaking. A teenaged, busted-out gambler coming home just in time for camp breakfast. No money in my pockets, no worries in my head. Enjoying the stunning morning air and light. Two years later my CCC camp would be an Army camp and we'd be at war. A lot more important things would happen to me, but I never forgot that night ride through the desert.

To begin at the beginning. A little history. The Mexicans owned that part of the country and the United States stole it from them. (Don't flinch at that *stole*—it was all for the best, after all. This book will make no moral judgments.)

Art in Vegas.

Anyway, in 1776 when the American Colonies were starting their fight against England for their freedom, a Padre Escalante and his band of Spanish soldiers raised their country's flag over an oasis of green in the middle of a vast desert. They named it Las Vegas which in Spanish means "The Meadows." The Spanish who went north and discovered the mountainous part of the state, called the whole place Nevada which is Spanish for "snow-capped." There must not be a Spanish word for desert.

After we stole it from the Mexicans who had chased out the Spanish, Las Vegas was mostly inhabited by naked Paiutes addicted to long hours of rolling bones and colored sticks across the sand and putting up their wives and horses to back their judgment. (Could it be that the special climate and earth themselves nurture the gambling instinct in man?) Anyway in 1855 Brigham Young sent some of his best strong-arm boys from Salt Lake City, Utah, to Las Vegas to convert the Indians and make the area an agricultural wonder.

The Mormons at that time and in that place had a reputation for having green thumbs and bloody red trigger fingers but even they were no match for the hot sun and the gambling fever of the natives. After three years, the Mormons gave up and went back to Salt Lake City. It turns out they made a mistake because beneath that hot sand was untold wealth in gold and silver.

But in 1955, nearly a hundred years later, another Mormon, a young banker named E. Parry Thomas, left Salt Lake City and settled in Vegas. Whereas Brigham Young's green thumb and long rifles had failed to turn the desert oasis into anything worthwhile, E. Parry Thomas worked his financial black magic to transform the little town into a legendary metropolis that fascinates gamblers the world over.

Thomas came to Vegas as a small-time banker. But he had the vision and the nerve to risk enormous loans for the building of glamorous palaces in the desert. He is acknowledged in most circles as having been the most powerful prime mover in Vegas. (In the process he made a great deal of money for himself and his friends. His own personal fortune is estimated as well over $30 million.)

If you want to start any kind of business in Vegas, build a hotel, or get risk capital or huge loans. E. Parry Thomas is the man to see. He helped Howard Hughes acquire his hotel empire in Vegas and it is rumored he is one of few people ever to see Hughes in the flesh on Nevada soil. Thomas is also an architect of the social and community structure of Vegas. He devotes a great deal of his time to what is known as good works and has the honors to prove it—including being named "Man of the Year" by the Anti-Defamation League of B'nai B'rith.

WIN A CAR 25¢

LIVE TABLE GAMES
25¢ CRAPS 50¢ BLACKJACK
PENNY SLOTS
39¢ HOTDOG
44¢ HAMBURGER
GIFTS PACKAGE LIQUORS

KENNETH L. LEHMAN

FREE ASPIRIN &
TENDER SYMPATHY

What would have happened if he had come a hundred years earlier and been the man to deal with those gambling Indians? But better late than never. And it's sort of nice to know that Vegas came into full bloom because of a Mormon, finally.

In 1849 a lot of people fled from the East to California in the famous gold rush. They rushed so fast that they passed over the fabulous Comstock Lode in Nevada. That figured. People who join gold rushes are born gamblers and gamblers usually miss the boat. But in 1859 a few of these gamblers finally got lucky as gamblers sometimes do, and they fell into the Comstock Lode. And so a great many people finally came to rest in Nevada on a more or less permanent basis. Of course they chased the Indians right out of the desert.

By 1864 Nevada had about 40,000 citizens. They were still a territory and they hated federal rule. One of the federal laws awarded a district attorney a $100 bounty for every citizen he convicted of gambling. The people of Nevada wanted to become a state to get the federal government off its back and gamble in peace before most of its population wound up in jail.

They got bailed out by one of history's most sacred heroes who, alas, pulled a stunt right out of a crooked gambler's three-shell game. The man was Abraham Lincoln, President of the United States. In 1864 Lincoln needed the antislavery vote of the Nevada territory. According to existing law a territory needed 127,000 certified residents. Nevada had fewer than a third. Lincoln just told Congress to pass a special law, and it did. And so Nevada became a state. The whole deal was a little crooked but for a noble motive. Which establishes the premise that good things can come out of a little crookery. And if that is so, why hold it against Las Vegas that its fame and fortune were seeded by a reputed murderer and gangster named Bugsy Siegel?

The city of Las Vegas was officially founded on May 15, 1905, as a result of a public land auction by the Union Pacific Railroad. The railroad transported the rich of California free of charge to Las Vegas so they could squander their money buying worthless desert land. The Pacific Railroad sold lots for $1,500 and pocketed the money with the glee of a gypsy switch-handkerchief artist, never dreaming that these same lots would sell for a million dollars in the next fifty years.

But in those early days Vegas was just a vast expanse of desert surrounded by played-out gold and silver mines. There were no real natural resources that anyone could see. The only asset of the state of Nevada was the freewheeling attitude of its citizens. To put it more directly, they were gamblers and, in the Puritan sense of

CASINO

the word, *whoremasters*. That is, they allowed legalized prostitution and permitted gambling, legal and illegal. These so-called vices proved to be the salvation of the sovereign state of Nevada. Some of its present-day citizens may object to such terms but they should not. The plain fact is that the people of Nevada were far less hypocritical than the rest of the citizens of America and had a hell of a lot more common sense. There really was very little to do out there in the desert in the way of fun. Pauite Indians with their colored sticks and bones had been on the right track after all.

As early as 1879 gambling was legalized in licensed homes. Unlicensed homes simply paid off the law. Unfortunately everybody started to cheat, careers were ruined, lives were lost in disputes on how the Ace of Spades magically appeared when it shouldn't have. But after all why should the citizens of Nevada have been any different from the gamblers of ancient Rome and nineteenth-century England where the same things had happened with much more dire results. All through history, going back to 4000 BC, you couldn't get together a friendly crap game or a sociable night of cards without some sharpies trying to cheat. That has always been the big rap against gambling as an otherwise pleasant vice. Human nature ruined it.

The straight players could never match wits with sharpies and hustlers who loaded dice, marked cards, and used drugs and booze and women to beat the innocent gambler out of his bankroll. Things finally became so bad in Nevada that in 1909 members of the Women's Civic League rolled themselves into a huge rolling pin and put on the pressure to have gambling made illegal. So in 1910 to protect its citizens from the wrath of its women and cut down on homicides of welshing gamblers and errant husbands, the Nevada State Legislature passed a law against gambling. It lasted for just over twenty years.

For that twenty years the citizens of Nevada had to earn their livings growing crops in the sandy soil. They shot deer up around Reno and rabbits down around Vegas. They panned a little gold and raised a little livestock. They behaved themselves and didn't gamble except illegally. Anyway, they didn't gamble on the stock market because they didn't have enough money and they were too far away from New York. Some of the old-time degenerate gamblers actually bewailed their fate that they had not been taken to the cleaners by the great stock market crash of 1929. They claimed that they had been rooked by every other gaming device known to man—why did they have to miss the most fascinating and clever marked-deck hoax of all time? The Great Depression of the 1930s brought

4
QUEENS
CASINO
LUCKY LOUIES
ALL NEW FOR YOU
FREE SOUVENIR SLOTS
25,000 KENO
FOUR QUEENS
LUCKY LOUIES 24 HOUR RESTAURANT
HUGOS ROTISSERIE
FREE SOUVENIRS
CRAPS
BLACKJACK
ROULETTE

DUNES

PINS
"21"
CRAPS
COCKTAILS
JACK
"THE GOOD OLD DAYS"
25¢ HOT DOGS
5¢ BEER - 50¢ BAR DRINKS
25¢ DAILY SPECIAL
NOW!

POKER
SLOTS
PROGRESSIVE
SLOT JACKPOTS
NOW OVER $62,272.51
KENO 24-HRS
OPEN

MINT
HOTEL

citizens of Nevada back to their senses. They voted for legalized gambling.

How come our moralists don't bitch about the stock market? I bet craps, blackjack, keno, roulette, I bet basketball, football, baseball, boxing. I even lost $1,000 on a tennis match betting Bobby Riggs against Billie Jean King. (Male chauvinist father against women's lib daughter.) With horse racing I have a snobbish feeling against placing my fate in the hands of a noble animal, lovable and true, but controlled by men not so noble. With the stock market I feel the same way I once did gambling with a friend of mine who owned a marked deck. He promised not to "read" the markings when we played casino. He beat me ten games in a row. This astonished me. As a teenager I had won my neighborhood candy store in three days of solid casino playing. I went out and bought an unmarked deck and true enough won my money back. The stock market is the same. You give your money to a bunch of guys who have promised SEC they won't read the markings on the deck.

I once did a Wall Street guy, a broker, a favor. He told me to buy some stocks with a guarantee against loss. The stock immediately dived to the bottom. My broker sold the stock for the same price I had given for it. My question is whom did he sell it to and how?

Much has been made of the hazards of gambling dens, their ruin of honest hardworking people. Not enough has been made of the hazards of the business world. I personally would rather swim in a river full of crocodiles than go into any accepted legal business venture. This is not to me an unreasonable prejudice but is based on personal experience and observation of other people's forays into the wilds of democratic capitalism.

I have lost a great deal of money gambling. Late in life I decided to reform, to be respectable, to be intelligent and shrewd and responsible. Also I now had money and all of a sudden I acquired the cautiousness of the moneyed. Also their morality. My greatest desire was to outwit the federal and state tax laws.

A rich businessman friend offered the golden opportunity to come in on one of his gilt-edged, long-term real estate deals. It would save me a fortune in taxes. It would leave a great long-term estate for my children. It couldn't lose.

Well, he was a close friend and I trusted him. But I was no greenhorn just over on the boat. I hired a top accountant and a top lawyer. They investigated and negotiated the deal and assured me it was the opportunity of a lifetime. There was, of course, a little bit of a gamble. I *plunged* in.

Well, on that one legitimate, foolproof, common-sense action I lost more money than I lost in my whole lifetime of foolish gambling. And it was less

fun. I also had to pay for the accountant and lawyer, and their services in a foolproof deal never come cheap.

This doesn't mean that everybody should gamble instead of going into business. It could mean everyone should pay his taxes and to hell with it, even though that smacks of communism. One thing I'm sure of, I'd have been a lot happier if I had lost that money gambling rather than investing. Infantile, I know, and I hope to grow out of it. But until then, the hell with it. Give me a deck of cards instead of a tax shelter and I'll take my chances.

It's perhaps a commentary on our society and system of moral values that the only time the smart operators of the Vegas casinos got taken was through Wall Street.

A man named Alexander Guterma, a Russian born in Siberia, became a high-rolling gambler in Vegas. This may have been a dodge to become intimate with top executives of some of the Vegas hotels. He persuaded them to invest in his corporations and nearly stole the valuable Desert Inn through the manipulation of stock transfers of a razzle-dazzle corporation. It was only the street-wise shrewdness and cunning and instinct of points owner Moe Dalitz that saved the Desert Inn from being swallowed up by Guterma's scheme. But many of the Desert Inn executives lost personal fortunes and one Desert Inn executive was indicted. Guterma finally went to jail.

The Eastern banks and trust funds frown upon Vegas investments. Newspapers attacked the Teamsters Union for putting its Pension Fund into Vegas and yet it has not been proved that the Pension Fund has lost money by these investments. The charges that the Union men got payoffs for investing this money may be true. But anyone who knows banking and is brave enough to comment honestly will tell you that a great many banking loans are given with the inducement of some sort of reward for the official of the bank who approves the loan.

Just in recent history when New York City had its financial crisis, the Teachers Union led by Albert Shanker pledged its Pension Fund as a loan to the city to prevent it from going bankrupt. One only had to see the newspaper photograph of Mr. Shanker as he emerged from a "sit-down" with city officials to know that this "creditor" had been the victim of a very high-class mugging.

Horse racing is called the sport of kings and presumably is done to improve the breed. But to me betting on horse racing is the most degenerate form of gambling. By the time the tax people take their bite off the top you have a 20 percent "Edge" working against you. I don't know of anyone who believes that racing as a sport is

Craps—the true gambler's game.

PASS LINE
COME
FIELD
Don't Pass Bar
SIX
NINE
HORN
Any Craps
Hardway
8 FOR 1

completely honest. In fact, the only other betting sport that has a worse reputation is boxing.

Harness racing is so crooked, so blatant, that there have been instances of spectators rioting and trying to lynch the drivers. It's curious that so many moralistic attacks have been made on the gambling in Las Vegas which is to harness racing what Queen Victoria is to Messalina. Moral attacks are always curious. The New York financial establishment, the biggest and most competitive in the world, is reluctant to invest money in Nevada gaming and yet in New York the State Lottery had its operation temporarily suspended by Governor Hugh Carey because of irregularities. These irregularities were probably far more serious than has been reported in the press or explained by the officials of the straight-arrow New York political establishment. In New York 200 harness racing drivers are under indictment for fixing races and yet can sue to get their driving licenses back. In Nevada they would be forever barred.

But it took Nevada a long time to learn how to operate gambling. In the 1930s the Great Depression rolled in. Nevada was just sagebrush and exhausted gold and silver mines. The only thing working was illegal gambling on a grand scale with German bands in hotel lobbies, crap-tabled restaurants, and back rooms full of blackjack players. The officers of the law were getting rich from illegal payoffs.

So in 1931 the state legislature of Nevada legalized gambling once again. But it excluded lotteries, which was odd because a lot of the states permitted lotteries and so did a lot of countries that forbade other kinds of gambling.

Little knowing it would change the whole course of gambling history, that they were creating the most famous (remember, I'm not saying "great") city of the '70s, they passed laws to make sure they would get a fair hunk of the action. They got lucky too. In 1939 the federal government started building Hoover Dam and thousands of workers with big payday checks flooded the Vegas area. As the government barred gambling in the work area, Vegas was the nearest "Big City."

The state of Nevada permitted certain individuals to open up gambling casinos. But these lucky fellows had to pay a tax to the local sheriff and county commissioners. According to law such moneys went into the public treasury. In 1947 Nevada passed another law. You had to get an okay from the State Tax Commission of seven good men tried and true. Only the good guys were licensed. Bad guys could no longer shop from county to county to find a bribe-taking official.

Now only the straight people could get in, they hoped. Also in 1947 a 1 percent gross tax was imposed. A gross tax could not be beat with any chicanery. The state had to get its money. The casino operators could not pull the tax avoidance gimmicks that big outfits like General Motors or respectable billionaires like the Rockefellers engineered. You can't beat gross taxes. The casino operators and the state of Nevada became partners. That first year Nevada collected a hundred grand which means that the casino guys made ten million. So in 1947 Nevada upped the gross tax to 2 percent. It also slapped a license fee for each table a casino operated. They counted all the tables—blackjack, craps, roulette, baccarat, poker, etc. The take was over 700 grand which meant that the casino operators had taken in over $35 million. The desert was blooming.

Before the war Reno was *the* gambling town in Nevada, but it was far more famous for quick divorces. After World War II the big action shifted to Vegas. There were two reasons for this. Number one, Vegas was closer to Los Angeles. And number two, a man named Bugsy Siegel discovered Vegas.

The legend of Bugsy Siegel is familiar. A big-time mobster/hitman in Brooklyn, he escaped the electric chair by the skin of his movie-dentist-capped teeth and decided to move west. Driving through the desert he came upon the dusty city of Las Vegas with its small bar and casino business and had a vision. He would build a Xanadu according to Hoyle and millions would flock to the promised land. He saw himself as a new Moses (and in fact later thereafter was sometimes spoken of, not to his face, familiarly as "Murdering Moses").

But the truth is somewhat different. Originally Siegel had gone west to become an actor. George Raft was a buddy he borrowed money from and used to gain entry into the movie world. Like many underworld figures Siegel had a great deal of charm to go with a brazen confidence in his own worth. He had a handsome open face but no talent. He couldn't even play a gangster. However, he made some good money hustles and also scored sexually with box office movie stars. Most Hollywood people did not know his background, strange as this may seem to people who do not understand the peculiar insularity of the movie world. The few people who did know were attracted rather than repelled by Siegel's reputation. Jean Harlow became the godmother of Siegel's two daughters.

In California, Siegel worked for the Eastern mobs in their struggle for control of the racing wire to the West Coast. He eventually succeeded, because some of the West Coast boys died suddenly. As part of his duties

*Blackjack—
the amateur's game.*

HORSESHOE
HORSESHOE
HORSESHOE

Siegel went to Vegas often. Even then during World War II Vegas had some plush hotels that were doing well. Siegel had studied the Vegas area pretty good and spent a lot of time figuring before he dramatically announced his "discovery."

The story of how Bugsy Siegel built the Flamingo Hotel has been told so often that only a fast recap is necessary. Siegel used all his mob and movie connections to get money and materials to build the flashiest and poshest hotel in America. He wanted the hotel to be legendary. This was in postwar 1945 and building materials were impossible to get. He used black market. He used movie studio material quotas. Senator Pat McCarran helped.

Siegel was a peasant building his house to last for generations. He had the foundations made extra, extra strong; it may be the strongest hotel ever built in the desert anywhere. Siegel wanted it built quick. Del Webb, the builder, said okay but wanted his money at the end of every working day. Siegel gave it to him. Siegel also arranged for the scarce materials to be delivered. But despite his awesome reputation everybody stole from Siegel. The truck drivers who delivered building materials in the morning drove back in the darkness of night to steal them and deliver them again the next morning. One driver claimed they didn't do it to get rich. But since materials were hard to get, they were afraid to tell Siegel they couldn't deliver. They were afraid he would kill them for holding out. So they stole it from him, delivered it to him the next day to avoid his wrath, and only incidentally to make a few bucks.

Siegel also hired the best interior decorator in the West. This gentleman marveled at the huge stockpiles of cement Siegel had acquired despite severe postwar government restrictions. "Yeah," Siegel said. "I need a lot. But if I don't like your decoration I'll save a little of it for you." The interior decorator immediately made plans to leave for points unknown until Siegel convinced him he was kidding.

Just as Siegel built the Flamingo Hotel as a peasant builds a home in which succeeding generations would live, the so-called mob guys and professional gamblers like Moe Dalitz and Major Riddle did the same. Others followed. Notice that *so-called.* I would no more call them such names than I would call President Ford a crook for pardoning Nixon, or a banker a thief because his bank fails, or a legally licensed personal finance company a Shylock.

Siegel and his Flamingo Hotel proved to be an unlucky combination. The casino in the Flamingo lost big money chunks to gamblers. Siegel had very paranoid secret partners. Also very tough. In 1946 Siegel drove to his home in Beverly Hills to spend a few relaxing days with his Hollywood buddies and girlfriends. In the dark outside his home an unknown gunman leveled a carbine and blew the window out. Then blew Siegel's head apart.

From then on the Flamingo became a moneymaker. The joke in Vegas was that Siegel was killed not because he was dishonest but because he was unlucky. In any case, the Flamingo had proved there was a market for Xanadus in the desert.

The shooting of Siegel set off alarm bells in Vegas. There were rumblings from Washington of a federal law to bar gambling casinos, a replica of the Prohibition laws. The citizens grumbled. The Nevada legislature took immediate steps to clean house before somebody else did it for them.

Remember that many of the gambling entrepreneurs who started Vegas had violated their social contract. Because they broke the laws against gambling (and maybe a few others). As owners of illegal gambling operations they were outsiders in the worlds they lived in. But Vegas gave them their legal world. They could function finally as members of the social order. They could renew their social contract. It is no accident that they brought their families, that they settled in, that they became part of the community. For the first time in their lives they fulfilled their part in the contract that every human being must have with the society he lives in. Must, if he is to live what is called a normal life. Under the influence of these men Las Vegas became a more structured, lawful society despite the influx of gambling degenerates from all over the world. Schools sprang up. Universities expanded. Tourism exploded.

It is true that the churches were built as payment to blackmail. Church groups, in the beginning, attacked gambling ferociously. The gambling wheels of Vegas got worried. The most important fact was that gambling could always be wiped out in any state election by the citizens of Nevada. The gambling bosses solved the problem in the same way they had solved law problems in other states where gambling was illegal. They bought up the opposition or seduced it. In Vegas they poured in the money to support the churches. They built churches of every faith. Baptist, Catholic, Mormon, Shinto, anything. They filled up the charity community chests to overflowing. They cleaned up the surface of Vegas so that it looked like a sparkling-clean city. Stickup artists and muggers were moved on by force, prostitutes were channeled into business routes which shielded them from any public exposure. Gangland killings were prohibited (nobody could stop the eternal slaughtering of loving spouses).

Gambling games were mostly straight in Vegas. Losers were treated gently and given air and bus fares home plus eating money. Customers were protected as much as possible from the con men, the greedy thieving prostitutes, by stronger action than the law allowed. Blackmail was rare despite the claims made in that famous book *The Green Felt Jungle*. Here let me say that I read that book with complete fascination before I got to know Vegas. It is an all-out attack on gambling and the city but instead of my being repelled it made me more determined to go there. I think this was true of most readers. And though I have no reason to doubt the truth of the book (its authors were far more knowledgeable than I), still I must say I have never in fifteen years experienced a cheating or blackmail incident in Las Vegas.

Today the city of Las Vegas, Nevada, is the greatest, most popular, most luxurious, most honest gambling center the world has ever known. It's easy to make a statement like that—but how to back it up? And how *not* to make it sound sycophantic? Are the Vegas fathers paying me off? This is by no means an insulting question. The whole history of gambling is filled with chicanery and complex double-dealing. The social structure is riddled with bribery on all levels. So rather than feel insulted by such a question I hereby take an oath that I'm not being paid off. I hereby affirm and assert that I even owe a fortune in markers to the casinos, every penny of which they have won fair and square. I hereby assert that I can no longer sign markers in Vegas because my credit is not that good there. True, I'm in their debt. But the day they cut off my credit and made me pay cash for chips was the day I finally broke my gambling habit. So I owe them a debt of gratitude. I will pay off that debt of gratitude by trying to show that Vegas gambling is mostly honest.

Las Vegas is, psychologically, the most dangerous place to gamble. The casinos are open twenty-four hours a day. They have the most sophisticated method of extending credit. They give you free drinks, free food, free shows with the most popular stars in the world, they give you beautiful girls. The Strip where most of the super-luxury hotels are has more neon lighting than fabulous Broadway ever dreamed of. Buy a couple of grand in chips and you are treated with the respect of nobility in France or England. You are Duke for a day, a Lord for a week.

Vegas casinos have a mistlike, fairytale quality about them. Air and natural light are shielded away from gamblers so as not to distract them. Time is dismissed. There are no clocks visible anywhere. You are a sleeping beauty waiting for the prince of good fortune. It is not too important that your pockets are being emptied while you

PASS LINE
4
8
NINE
10

dream. You are glad to pay the price. You may even feel you are getting a bargain. And if you can win—AH.

At night the scene is vulgarly breathtaking. There is this small city lit up with millions, literally millions of dollars of neon lighting surrounded by desert. On the horizon forming an almost perfect circle around the city are blue-black mountains to close the magic ring. After a good free dinner with brandy, what a childlike feeling of pleasure it is when you saunter down the Strip breathing in the desert air, seeing the great names of Frank Sinatra, Buddy Hackett, Don Rickles, Ann-Margret, Shirley MacLaine emblazoned in gold and red on electric signs four stories high. But remember, after three days it all turns into a pumpkin.

You have your choice of casinos, the gold and white togas of Caesar's Palace, the stylish, bluish Tropicana casino, the deeper red plush of MGM, the chandeliered Hilton. Or you can go into downtown Vegas, Glitter Gulch, the Western garter girl garish of the Four Queens, The Golden Nugget, Binion's Horseshoe, and The Mint. You carry inside you the hope, the fierce desire that not only is this all free, but that you will win *their* money. Who could ask for anything more? Dreamers come from Japan, Araby, India, the Argentine, Mexico, Estonia, from Los Angeles, and all of the United States. It is a great bargain but not as great as it used to be.

Back in 1947 you could catch an 8 P.M. show for the bargain price of $3.50. You got a big first-class dinner in a plush showroom, a topnotch entertainer like Frank Sinatra plus supporting acts. The midnight show (a pop singer, a mildly risqué comedian, a famous band) was yours just for buying a sixty-five-cent drink. And that was at the plush places on the Strip.

In 1976 an ad in the *Los Angeles Times* advertised a room and meals for $9.95 a day that included free bacon and eggs (as many times as you want), free TV, free local calls, free coffee, and snacks. But not at the plush Strip hotels. Today on the Strip, at the fancy hotels, there are no such fantastic bargains. But the price of an evening's entertainment and a meal is still a good buy and if you are a big gambler you can get "comped," courtesy of the house.

Statistics have been compiled, surveys made. I distrust both, but personal observation sort of makes me believe Vegas statistics are mostly true. (Remember everything connected with gambling is suspect. But you might say this about politics, the stock market, and even banking.)

Anyway 96 percent of the people who go to Vegas say they enjoyed their visit. A very interesting statistic because it is certain that 90 percent of

BUST!!

the visitors to Vegas leave as losers. No sweat, the customers are loyal. Of those interviewed, 30 percent claim they visit Vegas twice a year or more. (How can they afford it?) Average length of stay is four days. This has to be true. No gambler can afford to stay more than four days in Vegas. I love Vegas but after three days I'm dying to get out, and, economically, must.

Remember the longer you stay the less chance you have of winning. The house percentages keep working against you every minute. There is no beach, no interesting architecture, no medieval sectors to tour. Shopping is limited to hotel gift shops which have outrageous markups. You have to gamble. There are no alternatives.

Your best chance to win in Vegas is to fly in for one evening. Take the 5 P.M. plane from Los Angeles and leave Vegas on the midnight plane. To Hong Kong if necessary. I once had a big winning day in Vegas. I rushed to the airport. My plane caught fire on the ground. Foolishly I waited for another plane to New York. And it became another losing trip. I still can't believe it—the plane caught fire.

Typically enough Friday and Saturday are the heaviest days. Tuesday the lightest and this is logical. People have to go to work for the money they will lose gambling.

Why do they come? To "get away." For the shows and entertainment.

Winning is everything.

Nobody mentioned coming to win money which sort of proves that they are not really dummies. Hotels accommodate 56 percent and motels 34 percent. The other 10 percent presumably scrammed out of town with their winnings before it was time to go to bed.

Visitors spend an average of $67 a day EXCLUSIVE OF GAMBLING. (Airline visitors spend $75, bus visitors $35.) Also 55 percent of these visitors do not consider Vegas a good place to bring their children. A casino called Circus Circus tried to change their minds on this. The casino is ringed with Coney Island- and Disneyland-type arcades where kids can fool around. Circus acts go on above your head as you gamble in the casino. Personally I find it really unnerving to play a hand of blackjack as some guy in spangled tights goes flying over your head, gambling his way into a net. But the kids in the balconies above the Circus Circus casino seem to have a good time.

Astonishingly 26 percent of the visitors to Vegas are college graduates and 29 percent have a family income exceeding $25,000. Also 20 percent of the visitors are self-employed and probably gambling money they have skimmed off the top of their businesses, Vegas style. For what it's worth, skimming no longer goes on in Vegas. I think.

Another astonishing statistic to me is that in the average four-day stay, visitors only attended one and a half shows. Remember, these shows are top entertainers—real stars—and the fee to attend is comparatively cheap, often "comped" or free.

In 1975 over nine million people visited Las Vegas. A truly astonishing figure when you think that there is really not much to do there. The breakdown was Eastern, 13 percent; Midwestern, 19 percent; Southern, 12 percent; Western, 50 percent (this is what Siegel understood—Los Angeles would feed into Vegas). Foreign countries accounted for 6 percent—a deceiving figure, because foreign visitors bring a lot of black market money and are terrific gamblers.

Junkets and conventions bring in 13 percent of the visitors. The Convention Bureau even got a puritan Baptist religious group. One hotel owner wasn't too happy about that one. "They came with the Ten Commandments in one hand, a twenty-dollar bill in the other, and they never broke either one of them." In the year 1974 a total of 339 conventions booked into the city. For some it seemed like a weird choice as follows:

AMERICAN COLLEGE OF NUCLEAR PHYSICIANS
(Doctors have a big rep as gamblers. Casino shrinks claim it's because

doctors see so much human misery during the year they have to forget their troubles. Others claim doctors use it as a humbling experience because they have to play God in their work. And in Vegas God shows them how mortal they are.)

ASSOCIATION OF CHEFS (How do they eat the food?)

ALCOHOLICS ANONYMOUS—WESTERN SECTION
(Gambling is a great substitute for drinking. There is also a Gamblers Anonymous. When a gambler feels the urge he calls up a fellow gambler to come over and play gin rummy for matchsticks. [A joke.])

PEARL HARBOR SURVIVORS ASSOCIATION

SOCIETY FOR THE SCIENTIFIC STUDY OF SEX

SOUTHERN CALIFORNIA LEFT-HANDED GOLFERS ASSOCIATION

CLIPPED WINGS—UNITED AIRLINES STEWARDESSES ALUMNAE

FOURTH INTERNATIONAL CONVENTION OF ACUPUNCTURE

TRAUMA SEMINAR—AMERICAN COLLEGE OF SURGEONS

ICE SKATING INSTITUTE OF AMERICA

All these people have the use of 21,000 hotel rooms and 14,000 motel rooms. Rate occupancy is 15 percent to 25 percent higher than the rest of the hotels in the United States but this statistic is phony because a lot of those hotel rooms are given free to gamblers (comped).

The airport has a volume of a half million people per month traffic. I keep thinking of that incredible statistic because coming into Las Vegas you fly over endless miles of desert and then you come down into the heart of that desert and there is a neon city all by itself surrounded by sagebrush, rabbits, coyotes, and mountains. What the hell is it doing there and what does it really mean?

THE FUTURE "LAS VEGAS" ALL OVER THE UNITED STATES

In 1976 the citizens of New Jersey voted to legalize casino gambling in Atlantic City. In that same year the Federal Commission on the Review of the National Policy toward Gambling finished a three-year study and submitted it to Congress. Both actions indicate that the United States will soon become the foremost gambling country in the world. And that gambling will make taxpaying almost as painless as modern dentistry.

The commission recommended that the United States should have "the primary responsibility for determining what forms of gambling may legally take place within their borders." This means that the federal government will not pass a law—like prohibition—banning gambling throughout the

PLAY IN THE
WORLDS LARGEST CASINO
PAN

50,000.00
10,000
5,000
2,000
1,000
400
200
2
5,000
2,000
30,000
15,000
6,000
3,000
1,200
40,000
20,000
8,000
4,000
25,000
10,000
5,000
2,000
1,000
10
25,000
10,000
5,000
2,000
1,000
500

nation. Remember that for years a federal law hung like the sword of Damocles over the head of Nevada gambling.

The vote by the citizens of New Jersey indicates that more and more people are convinced that gambling could save their local economies. Atlantic City is a dying resort of huge decaying hotels on empty beaches. Many of its inhabitants are on welfare. There are no jobs, no industry. Legalized gambling should change this decaying town into another Las Vegas during the next twenty years. Unless greedy businessmen and venal politicians screw it up.

The Federal Gaming Commission gives Nevada high marks for its regulation of gambling. And the big concern about gambling in Atlantic City is how to keep the "mob" out. As Nevada now does. Well the mob is the least of their worries, or should be. For one thing, gambling has proved to be so profitable that the big business conglomerates would massacre the mob if it tried to move in. Big business in America has always been far more ruthless than our criminal elements.

The big danger is that the politicians will be so greedy for revenue that they will tax the gambling establishments right out of business. The federal commission recommends that all gambling winnings by individuals be made tax-free. For the simple reason that a tax-ridden gaming establishment

If you beat them, you can't hurt their feelings.

cannot compete with a parallel illegal gaming complex that is not taxed.

Another danger is markers or IOUs. If the politicians make these a legally collectible debt the resulting traumas may force the federal government to ban gambling on a nationwide level. It might happen that the casino owners of Atlantic City would wind up owning a good part of the individually owned businesses on the Eastern seaboard just by collecting markers. And then all you would need is evidence that everybody on welfare is gambling money in the casinos and signing away future welfare checks for markers.

Could welfare clients get credit at a gambling casino? If markers were legally collectible, most certainly. What more assured income than a welfare check? The whole government is behind it. So the smartest thing the New Jersey gambling administrators can do would be to follow in the footsteps of Nevada and rule that gambling debts are not legally collectible.

The Federal Gambling Commission states that its studies show the people of Nevada have more gamblers and gamble more of their income than the citizens of other states. Simply because gambling is more readily available. The commission also establishes that "regressive gambling" (which means that lower-income people proportionally spend more of their

CHAIRS FOR
BIG 6 PLAYERS ONLY

Hi, I'm
SUSAN
From
NEW YORK
Live It Up

money gambling than higher-income people do) is higher in Nevada. Again this is because of accessibility. The people who can least afford it will gamble most.

The classic example is lotteries. You can hardly call lotteries gambling. It is really a drowning man clutching at a straw. All those millions of people locked into jobs that will never make them even middle-class buy tickets as their one hope for salvation. Their one chance to escape a life of unremitting labor. That's not gambling—that's some sort of religious act.

Atlantic City will have to study Vegas closely to make its own operation successful. One of the greatest Vegas tricks is to make every gambler a king. If you have two thousand dollars to lose or even a thousand, you are treated like royalty. If you just throw the dice or step into a casino, you're at least a duchess. The customer is immediately ennobled, made a Knight of the Garter, a Chevalier of the Legion of Honor. It's a great feeling and millions of people will lose billions of dollars to taste it.

One of the biggest problems Atlantic City will have to face is that it has no desert encircling it to provide a *cordon sanitaire*. In Vegas, all would-be stickup artists of casino cages have no handy exit from the scene. In Atlantic City they can just melt into the woodwork of vast slums teeming with people. Atlantic City will have to worry about players getting mugged or blackmailed by pimps and prostitutes. The police organizations in the East do not seem to have the iron hand that the police of the West use so effectively. Atlantic City gambling casinos will have more trouble with the outside sharpshooters and hustlers working scams in their casinos. It must be said that the Eastern criminal seems to be more resourceful and have better political, judicial, and police protection than the wicked criminals of the West.

After the gambling victory in New Jersey, I read newspaper reports quoting Vegas wheels, most of whom claimed that Atlantic City casinos would not hurt business in Vegas. I consulted my own experts. They declare emphatically that gambling in Atlantic City will hurt Vegas: with one big IF. Atlantic City must build a comparable hotel plant and recreation facility. Atlantic City must import knowledgeable gambling executives. Atlantic City must create some sort of *cordon sanitaire*, an enclave, protected by police with special powers and judges who will understand that a cheating casino is as serious an offense as forging currency. It is obvious that an enormous capital investment must be made by the believers in our democratic capitalism. But there seems to be no problem there. The day after the voting that made gambling legal in Atlantic City the price of one grand hotel on the beach went from $2 million to $5 million dollars. The owners of take-out pizza joints are planning to expand into first-class restaurants. The citizens of Atlantic City celebrated as if another world war had just ended.

The reality is that there is no way for Atlantic City to fail. It will become a huge gambling Disneyland. And it will hurt Vegas to some degree but not fatally and certainly not in the near future. With the success of Atlantic City it is inevitable that other states will follow. New York will almost certainly legalize gambling in the Catskills resort area. Florida is another logical candidate. New York City may authorize exclusive gambling clubs in the English style. And not just for the tax money.

Consider that Las Vegas was just a little town of about 40,000 people and its population is now around 400,000. Think of the payrolls and the real estate values that came into being. On just payrolls alone, gambling generates $4 billion a year in Las Vegas. It creates billions of dollars in travel revenue, all those people flying and driving from the far corners of the United States and the world to get there to lose their money. Think of the food-processing plants it supports, the show biz people, the lawyers and the newspapers, the writers who write about it and other assorted hustlers, con men, and traveling girls. And of course some necessary infantile dreams.

For those who are disgusted by this vision of a gambling America, only a few consolations can be offered. It is not as destructive as war or as boring as pornography. It is not as immoral as business or as suicidal as watching television. And the percentages are better than religion.

It is of course completely wasteful and essentially damaging to a dynamic society that should further mankind. Nor can it maintain our strength against the ideologies of Russia and China. But that is neither here nor there. It will come and we can only hope that we will get lucky, singly or collectively.

A SHORT HISTORY OF GAMBLING

It is hard in this time of the atom bomb, permissive sex, the justification of drugs, to understand the horror of gambling expressed by so many social organizations, religious sects, and assorted judgment-makers. But a history of gambling justifies their horror.

The biggest and first crap game is mentioned in Greek mythology. Zeus, Poseidon, and Hades rolled dice for shares of the Universe.

Poseidon won the Oceans.

Hades won the Underworld.

Zeus won the Heavens and is suspected of having used loaded dice.

The second-biggest bet ever made, according to legend, is the god Mercury gambling at tables (whatever that means) with the Moon and winning from her the seventieth part of each of her illuminations which added up to five days. This is why the Earth has 365 days rather than 360. I note in passing that it is a He winning from a She, that no money passed hands, that no mention is made of what Mercury would have lost if the Moon had won. Or why Mercury thought the Earth needed another five days. (Maybe that's how "wishing for the moon" got its start.) But what the hell, it's just another gambling story.

The English word *gaming* comes from the Saxon word *gamen* which is defined as "joy, pleasure, sport." That's

one definition. Another definition is to play extravagantly for money. There was a period when gambling was as deadly and widespread a virus as the bubonic plague.

Centuries and centuries ago, man lived in a world that had few amusements as we know them today. There were no movies, no television, nor organized spectator sports leagues. Very few people could read. There was little music. What you had were booze, brothels, feast days that featured gladiators getting killed and churchmen in big churches telling everybody they would roast in hell. Gambling was the only real fun on tap anyplace, anytime. Its effects were worse than heroin today and more addictive.

All over the world people gambled anything. In Naples those singing gondoliers staked their liberty for a certain number of years for gambling debts. The Indians in the New World cut off their fingers to pay off a bet. They also had a crude form of roulette, spinning a stick and the person to whom it fell was the winner. In England a workingman was arrested for hanging another man. The man being hanged defended his hanger. He'd lost a bet and the stakes were that the winner could hang the loser. They had to bet something and all they had to bet was their lives.

Loser.

Loser.

Those fierce German warriors who destroyed the Roman Empire gambled their liberty on the throw of a dice and became the slaves of the winners. In China the rice paddy workers bet their ears and the losers sliced them off with a polite kowtow. In every age the gambling debt was a debt of honor and had to be paid.

In the eleventh century clergymen and bishops were fond of dice. What turned religion against gambling was the Crusades. Those Technicolor movies about the Holy Crusades never tell you that Richard the Lion-Hearted's army lost the war to Saladin because all those European soldiers were so busy gambling that they had no time to fight. The Turks on the other hand were forbidden by their religion to gamble. That is what is called a big "Edge." It got so bad that Richard and King Philip of France commanding the Crusader armies prohibited any soldier below the rank of knight from gambling. (I remember the same kind of law in the American Army during World War II. And there was George Washington.) The Crusaders' law was a little tougher though. Culprits were whipped naked through the army for three days. However, the two kings gambled like crazy. Big stakes. But the knights were not allowed to lose more than 20 shillings.

In Paris there was a game called hoca which working people were prohibited

Loser.

Winner.

from playing under penalty of death. That must have been some game.

In England during the 1700s many of the young aristocracy lost all their money and went to the Colonies to make a new fortune. The poor people gambled away their clothes and huddled naked in the corners of the gambling "hell."

General Edward Braddock came from an unlucky family. Not only did he have to surrender his army to the Americans, but his sister hanged herself because at the age of twenty-three she lost her inheritance gambling.

The English were crazy gamblers. In one night they lost sums equal to a million dollars in present-day purchasing power. Famous men such as Disraeli and Fox were heavy gamblers. This distribution of wealth was helped by professional gamblers expert at cheating. And if you didn't pay your gambling debts they challenged you to fight a duel. It was that simple.

Kings and emperors were sore losers and obnoxious winners. And crooked to boot. The Emperor Caligula lost all his ready-money treasury in a crap game, rushed into the streets, had two noblemen seized, accused them of treason, confiscated their wealth, and dashed back into the game. The Emperor Claudius had his carriages built especially to accommodate crap games and his coachmen had signals on when to gallop to turn over a bad roll. Even scholars were not immune. Aristotle wrote a learned essay on how to cheat at dice.

King Henry VIII of England was not only a tough guy with women but a reckless gambler. He lost the famous Jesus Bells, the greatest in England, which hung in the tower of St. Paul's Church. The guy who won them, a Sir Miles Partridge, made the mistake of collecting his bet. Those same bells rang in his ears when he was hanged a few years later for a "criminal" offense.

Nero didn't really fiddle while Rome was burning. He was shooting craps and losing. A lot of the Roman emperors were degenerate gamblers at dice. But the French kings later on were just as bad but a little more refined because cards had been discovered, so they lost at that. They also invented markers. (The Romans always played for cash and to this day Italian gamblers don't really trust markers or checks.)

Henry IV of France, rated as one of the great kings of France, was a degenerate gambler. He also was a crook. He used a professional gambler to cheat his nobles. Not for the money really but to make them so poor that it would weaken their political power. I guess you would call this some kind of détente. Anyway it helped Henry earn his reputation as a great king. Again rich people were allowed to ruin themselves but poor people were forbidden to gamble. Somebody had to do the work around the country.

When Charles V's army besieged the city of Orange, his commanding general gambled away the pay of his soldiers and had to surrender to the city he was besieging. Shortly thereafter, gaming was forbidden to the French cavalry under penalty of death.

The glorious Louis XIV cheated in gambling. And under Louis XV gambling became a raging plague in France. Everybody cheated. Loaded dice have been found in Pompei. Marked cards have been found in ancient English monasteries.

Somewhere along the line gambling became hooked up with health spas. In the 1700s women in France and England became heavy gamblers. In England a poet wrote, "She'll pawn her virtue to preserve her honor." Which I thought was a better idea than to let a guy hang you because he won the bet.

However, Greek and Roman women did not gamble, they had other troubles. The literary men of Greece and Rome did not gamble. The Russian writers (Dostoyevsky, etc.) were crazy gamblers. But there has been no great novel about gambling or gamblers.

It occurs to me now that Greek and Roman women did not gamble because in their time only dice existed. English and French women gambled because by that time cards had been invented. So in Vegas today you see very few women crap shooters. I guess because of this historical conditioning.

England has published a great deal of literature on gambling with case histories of famous gamblers and sharpers. These case histories usually end with the line "died of the pox (or a duel) at age twenty-five." So in the eighteenth and nineteenth centuries if you gambled you got venereal disease and died at an early age which should have discouraged young gamblers but most likely did not. It was a glamorous idea for a young Victorian puritan. Plenty of sex, plenty of fun and excitement. It was better than going to the Indian wilds of North America or the heat of India. Which leaves the question. Who the hell really did build the British Empire? Losers?

And then there is the famous question of suicide. Bust-out gamblers commit suicide. They really do. But is it gambling that causes suicide or losing? It is true that many men and women have ruined themselves gambling. It is true that they then killed themselves. But would they have done so in any case? One thing is clear. The English and French played for very big stakes. It wasn't gambling. It was a destructive war. To lose a thousand pounds at a single sitting was nothing for an English milord. Such a sum in the nineteenth century would support a working family for years.

Soft 17

In Spain gambling was used as a social entry. Wealthy widows of famous men used their houses as casinos. If you wanted to move in the best circles you had to gamble and lose. Winning was ill-mannered.

The religious establishment became involved in gambling right at the beginning and was mostly against it, because it was replacing religion.

Gambling has existed in every society from the most primitive to the most complex. Which sounds silly because you can say the same thing about sex. But maybe that's the point. The oldest known "rules" game in the Far East (23 BC) is "Go" discovered in Japan. This game involves hundreds of pieces representing various weapons of war armor. Given the Japanese culture at that time, this might almost be called a religious game. Dice were invented during the siege of Troy. India also has a claim to inventing dice because Indians established the first proof of how to cheat. Dice have been found in Egypt dating as early as 3000 BC. These early dice varied in size and shape from tiny, one-fifth of one inch, to bigger than golf balls. Dice were first used with board games like backgammon. The Egyptian Queen Hatasu (600 BC) has been found buried with an ivory astragal dice made of antelope bones and her twenty-piece draughtboard.

Gambling has been used as a religious command. How about those Greek and Roman priests studying the entrails of sheep? Sure they had a system, but who could know when the fix was in. Who picked the sheep or bull or whatever?

The Talmud equates a gambler with a thief. A gambler could not be a witness in any court of justice and was excluded from the magistracy.

In Africa the guilt of a woman accused of adultery was decided by letting her choose between two different bowls of water to put her hands in. One bowl had some sort of burning or marking essence.

The Greeks were least addicted to gambling and have left civilization with some of its greatest art and literature. The Greeks had severe penalties for gambling.

The ancient Jews resisted gambling until they came under the influence of the Romans. Then the Bible says that Moses was instructed by God to divide up the Promised Land by the use of a lottery. Which may have been the first case of church bingo and its inspiration.

When Rome became a great empire in 735 BC it spread gambling all over the world. Roman children were taught to gamble. The fall of Rome was attributed partly to the obsessive love of gambling by all people of all classes. (That I did the same with my own children strikes me as ominous.)

The counting rooms are watched by spies, the eye in the sky, and television.

SOFT COUNT

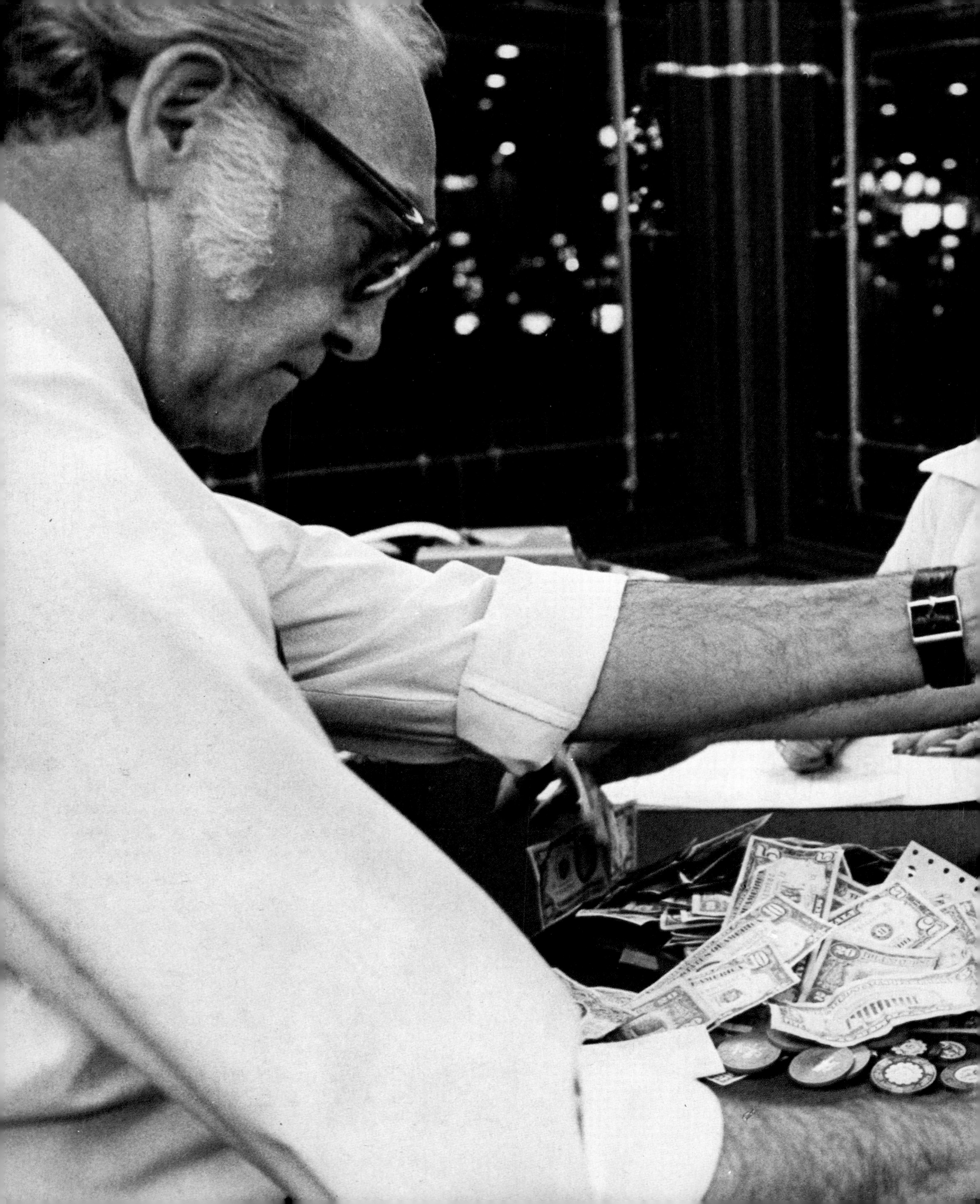

C-2
SW

More recently a man named Louis Cohen left a letter confessing that the great Chicago fire was not caused by that famous cow kicking over a lantern. He confessed that he and friends were shooting craps in the barn and accidentally started the fire. But he could have been just a bust-out gambler looking for a little glory. He would never steal the credit from a fellow gambler but gamblers don't care about cows.

Gambling can't take the rap for everything. The commander of the Spanish Armada forbade his sailors to gamble when they sailed against England. That didn't help.

Despite all this, religious leaders started coming down heavy on gambling. In the 1700s preachers gave famous sermons on the evils of gambling. They argued it was unfair to God to have him make decisions on all bets. (They forgot he was watching the feather from every sparrow.) But by then gambling had become so destructive to society that preachers had to clutch at straws. Working people stole from their masters. Professional gamblers seduced pretty housemaids and then talked them into absconding with the silverware. These types usually wound up on the gallows but not before they had the fun of losing the stolen goods at dice. The upper classes no longer worried about making their countries great, they were too busy rolling dice and dealing cards.

Finally there was a great revolution against gambling and it was wiped out comparatively by the simple expedient of making the government the bookmaker. The British came up with a great gimmick, the Premium Bond Lottery. In essence, you put your money into a savings bank and instead of getting the interest you got lottery tickets. Any money won on a government lottery was tax-free. The government kept the interest.

It was the French who invented pari-mutuel betting and the first office was opened in Paris in 1872. I had always thought pari-mutuels typically American.

The Romans invented lotteries. Iron Curtain countries have the same premium bond lotteries as does Great Britain.

Greyhound racing, which I always thought of as particularly English because of its enormous popularity there, was actually invented in America. In fact, the first patent was taken out in the United States in 1890 and the first track opened in Oklahoma in 1923. The first track in England was opened in Bellevue, Manchester, in 1925. And in 1943 I was billeted there as a soldier in World War II. There I met one of the many girls who worked as greyhound trainers and she told me that sometimes the girls masturbated the dogs to make them lose. I flinched and never tried to get inside information again. Another

This used to be your money.

proof, to me anyway, that I was not a degenerate gambler.

Reading the histories of gambling, one understands that the modus operandi of Vegas didn't come out of thin air. The gambling hells of England had free booze, free food, magnificent rooms to gamble in, all kinds of favors, including women.

The administrative and overseeing setups were very similar, with Shills, Pit Bosses and guards, Stickmen, Boxmen, Croupiers, etc. Even the percentages were the same. In the 1700s club owners figured to keep 25 percent of the money gambled. In Vegas they figure 18 percent to 20 percent.

Binion's Horseshoe Casino in Las Vegas displays $1,000,000 in cash. One hundred $10,000 bills, the last that are in circulation in this country. Binion's Horseshoe also has a couple of other very clever gimmicks. Binion was one of the founders of modern Vegas, one of its most picturesque characters. But he must have studied his gambling history. That display of $1,000,000 is a steal from a gambling hell of eighteenth-century London that displayed a fortune in gold to inspire the greed of degenerate gamblers.

Binion's Horseshoe Casino also takes over 500 photographs a day of customers admiring the million bucks in its showcase. Since the customer has to wait for the picture to be developed he naturally whiles away the time by dropping a few dollars at the gaming tables.

The Horseshoe also is the only casino that has a no-limit policy. In this sense the first bet that a customer makes when he walks up to the table is then his limit. For instance, though the usual limit is $2,000, if a gambler walks up and his first bet is $10,000, he can bet up to $10,000 in that betting session. This violates the cardinal casino rule that there must be a limit. That rule was established so that very rich gamblers would not be able to play a double-up system since such a bet would work most of the time if one did have the money to keep going higher and higher. But Binion's policy is very shrewd. That first bet in which he has the Edge almost insures the customer of starting in the hole.

From all my reading of the history of gambling from the beginning of civilization to the present, I must say that the present-day Vegas gambling is the most regulated and most honest that has ever existed. It is the best place for a gambler to get an even break. (The worst casino management to gamble against is a government agency. The people who run state lotteries are guilty of highway robbery. Not only do they take an enormous percentage of the sum wagered but then they tax the winner's winnings.

The whole government policy of taxing winnings without crediting losses is contemptible in every sense. If Vegas pulled that stuff the FBI and the lynch mobs would converge on the city like a nutcracker. It is not really gambling but placebo taxation.)

Europe's oldest gambling casino is Baden-Baden in Germany. Incidentally, Europeans gamble for much higher stakes than Americans. The plush trade there is more important than it is in Vegas. Also there is no European equivalent for the working-stiff trade that makes up a good part of Vegas and Nevada business.

In America the first gambling casinos were established on the Mississippi River. The famous showboat paddle wheelers. By 1833 there were about 500 in service and finally there were almost 2000, confirming that the Mississippi had to be broad. These floating casinos were every bit as lavish as the casinos in Vegas today but they were far more crooked. Many professional gamblers became millionaires with their cheating. Those who did not found a watery grave.

The American form of craps was not invented by black people of the American South. It is based on the famous game of Hazard which was the ruin of countless English noblemen. But the craps layout as used in Nevada has been changed in some of its details as recently as 1957. The changes were minor just to put in a few more sucker side bets. So craps is basically an English game.

The first roulette wheels appeared in Egypt and they had three zero slots for the house, making it even tougher to win. So it wasn't a French invention, though for the French it is the most popular casino game. (But with one 0.)

Slot machines were invented in 1895 by a young American mechanic, Charles Fay. He leased his first slot machine to a gambling saloon in San Francisco for one-half the profits. If he could have kept the patent on all the slots he would easily be the richest man in the world today.

In the same 1890 era New Orleans became the gaming capital of America and the state of Louisiana legalized gambling. But again gambling became so crooked gaming had to be made illegal.

The Louisiana Lottery of 1892 was so crooked that Congress made it a federal crime to transmit any lottery material through the U.S. mails, and thus indirectly gave birth to the great bootleg popularity of the Irish Sweepstakes in America in the 1930s and 1940s. It also gave birth to the Nevada trauma that the federal government would ban casino gambling. Some other states, Texas, California, and New Mexico, had legalized gambling through the years only to ban it again.

It seemed you couldn't keep crooks out of gambling. It was only with the success of Nevada gambling after World War II that legalized gambling got a new lease on life in the United States.

Britain made nearly all forms of gambling legal in 1960. So many little clubs sprang up that the British had to rewrite the laws to close some of them down. At one time the law was such that you could gamble at roulette without the house having an "Edge"; it banned the zero. I wondered how they could keep operating. I soon found out. In 1972, in a club in London, I hit a number for a big amount of money. The Croupier, a charming good-looking woman, scooped the ball out of its slot so quickly I didn't have a chance to protest as she announced another number the winner.

That is the only time, to my knowledge, that I have been cheated in a casino. Shortly thereafter the London club was closed. So I guess I wasn't the victim of anti-Americanism. They cheated everybody.

Now in England it is estimated that 75 percent of the people gamble at a per capita rate of £40 a year for every man, woman, and child. In the United States 75 percent of the people gamble and spend about $250 per person. In both countries gambling is the leading industry. If you count illegal bets.

During the last hundred years, in many countries the most powerful and respected men belonged to gambling clubs. The Duke of Wellington was a real winner. He not only defeated Napoleon, but as a member of the famous Crockford Gambling Club he never had a losing night. He just came for the food and booze. He never gambled.

Nearly everything I have ever read or been told about why people gamble is just plain bullshit. Some psychiatrists claim gambling is masochistic, that gamblers want to lose to punish themselves. Sure some do. Some people like to jump off the Empire State Building. But millions go up to look at the view. What is true is that there are guys who can win fifty or a hundred grand and not stop gambling and then wind up losing. They are known almost affectionately as degenerate gamblers. I was one on a small scale. (I once walked out of a Vegas gambling casino with ten grand cash.) My biggest win was $30,000 in baccarat but that didn't count because I owed the hotel markers so I just traded the cash in for my IOUs. But in my very worst days I was only a mildly degenerate gambler which gives me an understanding, I think, of the syndrome. It's not that you want to lose what you have won. It's just that you cannot believe it's possible to lose. When winning you are

Cream-of-the-crop student dealers on top.

A student learning to deal.

The Pit Boss and Slotman keep an eye on all the action.

convinced God loves you. You are convinced that some inner vision enables you to pick those numbers that were about to appear magically as the red dice came to a stop, as a dealer unlocked a blue-backed card.

A winning streak inspired a belief in your own infallibility. Why stop then? Also, what non-gamblers do not know is the feeling of *virtue* (there is no other word to describe it) when the dice roll as one commands. And that omniscient goodness when the card you need rises to the top of the deck to greet your delighted yet confident eyes. It is as close as I have ever come in my life to a religious feeling. Or to being a wonder-struck child.

In short, I wanted to win everything. Is that so different from those religious fanatics who dare to think that after death they will go to their particular heaven?

To those who find such feelings contemptible, I can only say that's how I feel about religion. No gambling hell deceives mankind so wickedly as religion deceives mankind about death. For it is our death that we continually try to escape. But what the hell kind of escape is gambling?

Why not political action to make a better world? Why not struggling harder to make life more successful? What about trying to appreciate the arts to make your life richer? All these are better and more satisfying alternatives. The only thing wrong with them is that many people don't choose them. It depends on your resources.

Gambling is not the right bargain to make in life. Nor drugs. I could even make a good argument against art. So many millions do not have the minds, the preparation to use art as an armor against life. Others have read too many books and come to a point where they despise knowledge.

How about careers and money? Many millions do not have the talent or pitiless cruelty for making money legitimately and do not have the merciless amorality to make money criminally. Come to think of it that merciless amorality helps legitimate money-makers. And then there are the physical endowments and, of course. old age.

How lonely old people are. How hard it is to make close friends. When you are past a certain age the juice to love your fellow man seems to evaporate. And we all know, no matter what our age, that younger people find older relatives burdensome.

And so it seems strange to me that writers and intellectuals single out old women playing slot machines in Vegas as objects to ridicule and use them as an example of our decadent society. Surely they, of all people, should know the meaning of pity. I take pleasure in seeing those old women intense as little children, waiting for cascading silver to fall into their laps, oblivious for those few hours to approaching death, the inability any longer to love truly. Yet they are reproached for not worrying about Vietnam, the coming atom bomb war, the destruction of the world's ecology, the pollution of the stratosphere.

Why should they give a fuck? They have lived their lives and they have paid their penalties.

Okay, maybe that's why old people gamble. But what about children? Here I can speak again from firsthand experience. I spent a good part of my childhood gambling. I taught my children to gamble at an early age. I'm an expert on why children gamble. Children gamble because they are greedy. They want to have everything, and are astonished when they don't get it. To me this is the most obvious characteristic of the gambler. It is a form of infantilism. And here again I must say that I don't think this is altogether bad in adults. It is a mistake to structure your life on a form of infantilism (a drastic mistake) but a little bit can help you get through life. Look at all the old guys playing touch football in the park instead of chasing twenty-year-old girls.

In my childhood I squeezed in a lot of card playing while becoming a sports hero on Tenth Avenue and reading Dostoyevsky at the age of thirteen. Before I even got into my teens (as a teenager I never listened to music, as an adult I love the teenagers' music), I was playing poker with very tough workingmen beneath lampposts in the streets of New York or in the backs of the local candy stores. Playing with local strong-arm punks and nickel-and-dime stickup artists, I had the infantile audacity to cheat. I dealt the Ace of Spades from the bottom of the deck; I stacked the cards, I went "light" in the stud poker pot.

I was an unskillful cheat. A simple cut would ruin my stacked deck but I would "forget" to offer the cards to be cut. My age placed me above suspicion. Later when I taught my children to play poker I never let them deal out the cards without cutting the deck. You can't trust kid gamblers.

In my childhood Christmastime, Christmas Eve was a time for all the family and relatives to play cards, it was one of the holiday treats. I did not know until I did research for this book that this is an ancient custom. Anti-gambling laws sprang up in Europe before Columbus discovered America. Remember it was in the 1400s that playing cards were introduced into Europe by some visitor from China. (Remember in China they were invented to keep concubines out of trouble.) Remember in some countries the penalty for gambling was death.

But for Christmas kings gave dispensation to the poor so that they could play at cards during the holiday season. In short they were permitted to enjoy the luxury of cards in celebration of the birth of Christ.

One of the indignities heaped on the American Indians was the constant cheating of them at cards by our honest pioneers. The desperate Indians manufactured their own playing cards made out of the skin of white men. It did not change their luck.

With childish single-mindedness I cheated my brothers at Christmastime. I was great at dealing myself the Ace of Spades from the bottom of the deck. I won a good portion of their Christmas envelopes received from uncles and aunts and godfathers. Not for the money; I just had to win. I can't remember what I did with the money. I think I treated them to sweets or bought them presents. I had to win because of the strange world that lay in the future, I think.

The great Roman Emperor Augustus played cards with children. Did he let them win? Did he let them cheat? In a Vittorio De Sica film, *The Gold of Naples,* there is a charming scene in which De Sica, a degenerate gambler, inveigles a child into playing cards. It must have come out of his experience because there are legends of De Sica gambling away the budgets of his movies before they were made. In an interview De Sica said, "Money has been my ruin." I'm guessing he meant that gambling was his ruin. And yet despite this infantilism he was easily one of the greatest artists of the cinema.

I think also card playing for children is a form of magic, of fairy tales. The delights and disappointments are monstrous. Dice do not fascinate children for some reason. Perhaps because there is physical motion exerted, there seems a cause and effect. Expensive toy games sold by stores for children are not in the same class. As a poverty-stricken father of five children I spent enormous sums on patented games dazzlingly boxed. My kids could be lured from these toys by the sound of a riffled deck of cards.

All parents should teach their children card games mainly because they are a great preparation for the disappointments of life. Once a child has drawn to an inside straight and missed, he will understand that life is not all peaches and cream. And when that same child loses a sure-fire pot with a pat hand he will understand that the future is full of nasty surprises. Also I think gambling keeps kids out of jail. I grew up in a tough neighborhood with a lot of opportunities to get into serious trouble. While some of my buddies were out late burglarizing and strong-arming, I was trying to break the candy store owner in casino.

Why do adolescents gamble? When I was in my teens I stayed out until 4 A.M. My mother screamed that I would be forced to marry the girl, that I would get her into trouble. I only wished she was right. I was too shy with girls to have any luck or any dates. I was out until 4 A.M. still trying to make my fortune in poker. But at least by this time I had stopped cheating altogether.

I stopped cheating because I was a star athlete and fancied myself a hero. I read books which said heroes did not cheat. I was better than anybody else. I knew it and I assumed the rest of the world knew it. I had the same attitude as French and English noblemen who considered themselves gentlemen because they did not cheat at gambling and who would commit suicide before refusing to repay a debt of honor lost at the tables. So I always paid my gambling debts. Thirty-five years later, no forty years later, I realize finally I am no better than anyone else. So I have left markers in Vegas I have not paid.

Meanwhile gambling (for nickels, dimes, and quarters) kept me out of jail. It made me forget for a few moments that my sex life was incomplete. It made me forget that a day of reckoning was fast approaching. The time when I would have to earn a living and support myself in a drudge job which I already knew I would hate. Sometimes at the enamel-topped card table at the back of a candy store I would think of stories I would write that would make me a rich and famous author. I never misled myself for a moment, even then, that I could make my fortune gambling. I was never more right.

World War II came and rescued me from the drudge job after only a year of suffering. Ask any soldier, sailor, or marine how he spent most of his time during World War II. Five days on a train from New York to Oklahoma I was resisting the temptation to deal the Ace of Spades from the bottom of the deck. Three weeks on a troop ship going to Europe I was honest but very lucky. A not-so-lucky paratrooper put a pistol to my head which taught me another valuable lesson. You have to be more careful when you are innocent than when you are guilty. I spent nearly four years in the wartime army and never fired a shot in anger. But I dealt a million hands of cards.

It was in a Southern training camp that I learned how to play blackjack. I lost my pay for six months. Then one day I noticed a sergeant throwing sealed decks of cards on each bunk. He saw me watching him and said genially, “The Red Cross gives them out.” I was only twenty-one years of age and still a hero, honest and unsuspicious. It was only later that I learned that the sergeant ordered specially manufactured marked decks from a firm in Chicago. His buddies then proceeded to wipe out the entire battalion payroll at friendly games of blackjack. The sergeant also would severely restrict weekend passes for his recruits. He didn't want them wasting their money in town on booze and women. It was after all his money.

It was in this same training camp that another soldier wanted me to be his confederate. He was the son of a Baptist minister who was also a crooked gambler. The father sent his son marked decks. He wanted me to be his partner. He would deal blackjack and I would play third base next to him and draw off bad cards that could make him lose. I refused his proposition. Star athletes on their way to becoming war heroes did not stoop to cheat.

It is possible to develop a better character through gambling. Here's how it works. In the heat of gambling you commit dishonest, treasonable acts. You betray the trust people have in you. You fail to fulfill obligations to those nearest and dearest to you. Then you feel so damn lousy about having done these things that you reform sooner or later (mostly later) and try to wash away your guilt by behaving honorably in all sorts of human situations. Or at least you try not ever to do that kind of thing again.

All of us have done things in our lives to be ashamed of, so it's nothing to

brag about. I have cheated at gambling in two periods of my life and I am still trying to wash the guilt away. I never cheated while I was winning. I only cheated when I was losing. Believe it or not there is a great difference between the two. To put it plainly, I cheated so that I could continue to gamble in that particular game, not to make money. I didn't want to be benched, an outsider while others played. However, I hold the strong belief that there is nothing lower in this world than a winner cheating, with the possible exception of a male politician voting against the legal right of women to abortion.

What possesses a group of mature people who know what life is all about to think that gambling can solve their problems? Desperation, that's what and something to put a little spice in your life.

One of the great untapped unnatural resources of this country is legal gambling on sports events. Conservative estimates on such wagering starts at $10 billion a year. Which is ridiculous. Peanuts. Let me give a logical progression that may strike some people as erratic but is completely convincing to me.

In the late 1950s I was a sports addict gambler. Or freak. I bet baseball, I bet basketball, and I bet football. We didn't have tennis then on TV or golfing or they weren't popular enough for a

betting line. The only thing I didn't really like was horse racing and I wasn't rich enough to play the stock market.

Okay. I was earning $120 a week as a government clerk. My fellow clerk was making $150 a week and he was a fellow gambler. Between us we bet at least $50 a day, every day, on one sporting event or another. We averaged $300 a week or at least $15,000 a year in bets. Of course we didn't lose all that money—sometimes we won. But the bookmaker figures to keep 10 percent of all money bet so he earned $1,500 a year. In this affluent democracy there had to be at least a million guys like us. Now the total amount bet is $15 billion. Of which, if everything breaks out right, the bookmaker holds $1.5 billion. But the truth is that there were at least 10 million sports bettors who bet as much or more (they certainly earned more money than we did, though we may have been more degenerate), so multiply everything by ten and you have $150 billion bet with a $15 billion hold by the bookmaker. Now that was in the 1950s. Today the guy holding the job I had is probably earning $200 or $300 a week. So double the $150 billion and you have $300 billion. *Plus,* and this is a big plus, the TV set has made maniac sports fans out of countless more millions of Americans, including a lot of women who never bet before. So the figure is even higher.

Okay. Ridiculous. Impossible. Three hundred billion dollars cannot be wagered under the table. The hell with it. Nobody really knows. Let's talk about a scenario in which gambling on sports in the United States is made legal. Let's talk about the money first and worry about the moral implications later. After all, this is America and free enterprise.

Let's take one sports event. The football Super Bowl event.
Fifty million people watch the Super Bowl. Let's be conservative. Some people will bet, some people will not, but the bets will average out to $10 a viewer which comes out half a billion dollars gambled on this one event. And if anyone doubts that, ask any syndicate gent how much he would pay to have the franchise for that one event.

Then how about the World Series? Easily another half billion. EASY. Then how about the divisional titles in both sports? HOW ABOUT THE THOUSANDS OF BASEBALL GAMES DURING THE REGULAR SEASON? How about the hundreds of professional football games each season? How about the thousands of college football games? We don't even have to bother about basketball, tennis, and golf and what I consider a real dark horse, jai alai. How about that real blockbuster, the Olympics?

Illegal bookmakers in America today take bets on all these games and events except the Olympics. But they can't advertise and everybody knows the magical effect advertising has on sales. So let me make a prediction. I'm ashamed even to put this down on paper it is so outrageous. Remember this figure is the amount bet, not what the bookmaker makes. Okay, the total amount that will be wagered on sports in the United States of America if that betting were made legal would be: ONE TRILLION DOLLARS.

I've said it and I'm glad. If Uncle Sam were the bookmaker he'd keep 10 percent of this which would come out to 100 billion dollars. (Imagine if he Shylocked the losers.) Assuming conservatively that the politicians running it would steal half this, administration costs, thousands of political plum jobs, CIA and Pentagon skimming—still that leaves a profit of $50 billion.

As I write this I know it is true. And I know how the Wright brothers felt when they said they could fly.

Never mind about a lousy $100 billion a year. We are, after all, a civilized society. There are morals involved here. A whole culture could be at stake. And the owners of our professional sports teams are so concerned about these issues that they oppose any legislation to legalize gambling on sporting events. They make the argument that wicked, crooked gamblers will ruin the integrity

of the game by trying to put in the *fix*. Youthful athletes will be corrupted by numbered Swiss bank accounts and Las Vegas dancing girls. And when this happens, Americans will lose their faith in the integrity of sports and fall into complete moral decay and destroy our democratic system. (They never mention that sports fans may become degenerate gamblers and ruin themselves.)

Everything they say will happen could possibly happen. But if American sports fans have weathered professional team owners all these years, they are made of very strong stuff indeed. The rapaciousness and willfulness of sports club owners have no parallel in our industrial society in the last half of the twentieth century and few equals in the first half of this century. Their concern for the youth of America would have inspired Molière. Not since slavery was abolished have bosses treated their employees with the contempt for human beings, as chattels, as the owners of professional sports clubs treated their players. Until recent times owners actually refused to talk to players who were represented by an agent or lawyer in negotiations for their services. The history of the greed of club owners is too well known to go into again. It must be assumed that their concern is monetary rather than moral. They are laying the groundwork to get a piece of the gambling profits.

It is true that some players will be bribed. It is true that some games will be fixed. It is true that the almost religious fervor of the sports fan will be traumatized by occasional scandals. Well, that's life. We've fought wars in Asia, turned over governments in South America, had hundreds of thousands of young Americans killed and wounded by real bullets and bombs. And that was for less than a trillion dollars. We've had a President and Vice President who resigned in disgrace in the 1970s and over fifty million Americans still went out to vote. You just can't discourage an American fan. Let's assume the worst happens. Let's say, Almighty God forbid, that somebody fixed the Super Bowl game. What would happen? Well, one football team would have lost to another football team, that's all. The fans wouldn't even lose their money. The only ones who would get hurt would be the bookmakers. Because a fix is a conspiracy to get the bookmaker's money, not the gambler's. No matter who wins or loses the game, half the bettors will lose and half the fans will win. The bookmaker gets hurt but that will be mere pilferage considering the overall sums involved. And besides we can always protect them the way we protect cigarette smokers. Just put signs up in all betting parlors, signs that read like the ones on cigarette packages that say you may get cancer. (And tobacco doesn't come close to a trillion gross, $100 billion net.) Sure 100 million Americans will be deceived. It won't be the first time.

And what's all the fuss about? Fixing a ball game is not rape, it is not murder, it is not even being a Communist. It falls in very nicely with our laissez-faire democratic capitalism of letting prices and wages find their own level and the classic "let the buyer beware." Thinking it over very carefully, I believe I would be less ashamed of my sons' throwing a ball game than if they went into banking, selling insurance, or bossing a movie studio. Though there's nothing to be ashamed of in those rackets either. It's just a question of degree.

TV moguls already tamper with the integrity of the game, though indirectly. There are stories that in one Super Bowl game the referees decided not to call offensive holding penalties—in order to speed up the game for TV viewers. Such a decision is worth 7 points for the team with the better passing game.

And I can't wait to see what the advertising agencies will do to promote gambling on sports. Maybe we'll see O.J. Simpson winking at us and saying, "Tap out on Buffalo, I feel strong." Or Muhammad Ali giving us a little poem just before his next big fight.

> Go out and hock the family jewels,
> I'll make that boy look like a fool,
> I'll hit him once and I'll hit him twice
> And put that fool right back on ice.

Or better still an appeal to greed. On the TV screen we will see a huge stack of hundred-dollar bills with the legend "This could all be yours. GAMBLE."

That never fails.

When the Dodgers and Giants moved to the West Coast they screwed up the sleeping habits of hundreds of thousands of men on the East Coast and maybe even broke up some marriages because the West Coast games started at 11 P.M. and you had to stay up until 2 A.M. or 3 A.M. to sweat out the results of the game and know whether you were a winner or a loser. Sometimes your wife, impatient, made you a loser anyway. There was a fine line to walk. Did you go to bed with your wife, make love, wait for her to fall asleep, then tune in for the last few innings? If you did that you were a nervous and sometimes impotent lover.

In any case, sports betting makes for a hectic day. In the morning at work I picked afternoon baseball bets. During lunch hour I ran uptown to see the bookmaker. During the afternoon I picked night bets and before I went home to supper I dropped in to see my Shylock if I had been a loser in the afternoon. Then I went to see the bookmaker. Sometimes I went to the night harness racing. It was exhausting. Do you ask where did I get all this money? You may well ask. I went into debt. I finally had to give it all up because I had no time to write and I was trying to finish a novel. Oddly enough it never occurred to me to write about gambling in those days.

At the age of thirty-five I gave up gambling. I resumed ten years later in Las Vegas but stuck to casino gambling. Never again head to head.

But still one of the great days of my life, one that I will never forget was when I took my oldest kid to the Polo Grounds to watch the Giants play the Dodgers. The Giants won and my son and I were both overjoyed. My emotion was less pure than his. I had the Giants bet in a three-way parlay and as we walked on the deep green playing field toward the exit, part of a happy throng, I looked up at the scoreboard and saw that all my bets had won. I had picked every game right that day. It was a Sunday, no night games. The amplifying system played a joyous victory march and I was rich. I had made nearly a thousand dollars, a fortune for me in the 1950s. I would not have to borrow money to buy clothes for my kids when they started school in the autumn. I did not gamble that money away. I was not a degenerate gambler.

Another time I had to move my family to the Bronx into a new housing project. It cost $85 to move. I only had $20. I bet the $20 on a baseball parlay taking two underdogs with big odds. I won. I didn't have to borrow the money. I kept my pride.

What if I had lost? Well then I'd borrow. But I was no worse off than before. My creditor would be worse off since I would have to borrow $85 rather than $65. And that's how a gambler's mind works.

THE HONESTY OF GAMBLING IN VEGAS

Hi, I'm
KAREN
From
WASH.
Live It Up

Hi, I'm
MONICA
From
ILLINOIS
Live it Up

HORSESHOE
$1,000,000.00

The most frequently asked question about Vegas concerns the honesty of the games. I used to wonder about that especially because I was such a consistent loser and I thought myself an expert gambler. And the whole recorded history of gambling in every civilization shows that when you have gambling you have cheating.

Well I'm naturally paranoid. When I play cards with my kids I always cut the deck. I can't trust anyone to sign my checks or have control over my business affairs. All gamblers are paranoid, though they call it superstition. I know a gambler who, when his wife had her third child, suspected her of having an affair with the resident doctor during the three days when she was recovering from childbirth. That's gamblers. But now, after fifteen years of watching and trying to figure out how they cheat, I reluctantly come to the conclusion that Vegas has honest casino gambling and it may be the first time in the history of civilization that gaming houses have been run straight.

Of course most Casino Managers in their hearts are as crooked as stock market brokers. But they bank on the house percentages, and the state of Nevada has some very tough laws plus very close policing. Another reason the casinos are straight is the same reason that a store like Bloomingdale's has to give you good merchandise. It needs repeat business. It cannot jeopardize a huge capital investment.

The gambling "plant" of Vegas—the combined worth of the hotels and recreation areas—figures out to a billion dollars. For 1975 Clark County casinos (Las Vegas) reported winnings of $771,500,000. That's over three-quarters of a billion dollars. For the whole state of Nevada winnings totaled one billion and one hundred million dollars. (Spelled out is more impressive than a row of numbers.)

Now if they can win all that money honestly why fool around and louse it up? Plus why give crooked accomplices a blackmail hold over you? If you lose your license you lose your 10-100-million-dollar plant or hotel.

Talking to gambling executives on the operating level, many of whom started in illegal gambling, you learn the following: That the illegal gambling clubs had to cheat because their political and police payoffs were so high, far less than the taxes imposed legally by the state of Nevada. Gambling joint owners knew even then that it was better to run an honest game because then you got customers coming back for more. When you cheated and hustled, you turned people off gambling. Vegas gives a gambling service that makes gamblers feel that they get a fair shake and maybe even more than their money's worth.

The fabulous Binions—at the only casino that lets you set your own limit.

Kentucky Derby

Racing Form
Kentucky Derby Matches 9

Meanwhile the Nevada State Gaming people keep an eagle eye on casinos which is not to say a casino can't cheat you if it wants to or that maybe in the beginning there wasn't some "bail out" cheating or that even now there may even be some dirty work at the minor crossroads of small joints in the sticks.

A Vegas hotel owner must know the basic facts of life about gambling show biz. He must know that Frank Sinatra will raise the "drop" of the casino more than any other entertainer. He must know that Elvis Presley is the biggest entertainment draw in the history of Vegas but has no appeal for "premium" high-rolling customers. He must know that Barbra Streisand is a flop as a gambling draw. He must know that you need a lot of customers to fill a gambling casino. A hotel with 1,000 rooms, two people in each room, gives you 2,000 people.

At your gambling tables say you have room for 500 people. The 4-1 ratio is not a good one simply because people do not gamble twenty-four hours a day and not all people gamble.

The hotels in Vegas are now almost entirely owned by conglomerates. The old-time barons of gambling are gone. If you can believe the stories about Vegas this was accomplished in the finest tradition of American democratic capitalism. As the gaming in Vegas acquired a reputation for honesty and the business became more respectable, as the projection for expansion became more optimistic, big American business wanted a piece of the action.

The politicians in Vegas were agreeable. They wanted to see the original innovators with their suspicious ties to the mobs eliminated from the gambling scene. The story goes that J. Edgar Hoover and his FBI attacked on one flank and Howard Hughes and the conglomerates attacked on the other. The founding fathers of gambling in Las Vegas were told they had to sell or the FBI would start leaning on them very hard. Again reason prevailed so the story goes. Fair prices were to be paid but there was to be no haggling. There is a story about one large hotel that received an offer from either Howard Hughes or one of the conglomerates and was told that he had twenty-four hours to make a decision or else. They sold and Nevada became "clean." Who says capitalism doesn't work?

The success of any Vegas hotel depends on the success of the casino, its volume and winnings. The Casino Manager is the most important executive in the hotel's gambling operation. He has to be charming, he has to be smart. Never mind smart, he has to be Sherlock Holmes and if he is not honest, all is lost.

A retired faro Dealer. They don't deal faro in Vegas anymore.

The Casino Manager in Vegas today is usually a man in his middle years with at least twenty or thirty years' experience in gambling. Some of them in their younger days ran illegal gambling in different cities in the United States. Some of them were Dealers who were not above stealing a little, as they will freely admit.

The Casino Manager's primary job is to guard the sacred bankroll of the casino. He must control the Cashier's Cage. He has the final word on credit given to customers. He can fire any casino employee without appeal.

The Dealers and other gambling executives are the only workers in Vegas who are not represented by a union. The hotels will not budge an inch. The reason for this is simple. They feel that a union will give the Dealer a license to steal. With a union chicanery would have to be proved. Under the present setup Dealers can be fired just on suspicion. The Casino Boss will tell you that gambling cannot operate if the Dealers are organized into a union. For instance, in a court of law, if a blackjack Dealer gets terribly unlucky, and his table keeps losing fifteen nights in a row, there is no legal proof that he is cheating for the benefit of an "outside" man or "crossroader," that he is "dumping out." But a Casino Manager knows that by all the laws of gambling percentages such continuous losing is not possible unless the Dealer is crooked, and so he fires him.

The Casino Manager appoints the Shift Boss, the Pit Bosses, and the baccarat "Ladderman" who are all responsible directly to him.

The Casino Manager must also play the role of affable Host to customers; he must train each employee to be warm, charming, and a "professional friend." He must train his employees to "root" for the customer without helping him.

The Casino Manager and his personnel must know that gamblers sitting in wheelchairs are suspect because they can get a view of the Dealer's hole card. The Casino Manager must use the "eye in the sky" and closed circuit television to make sure his personnel remain honest.

The Casino Manager has to have the most suspicious eye in the world.

Does a Dealer walk funny? He may be slipping chips into his shoes. Is he too charming with certain customers and "dumping out"? Is he careless counting change to the detriment of the House? The Casino Manager trusts nobody.

All Dealers must wear narrow ties so they cannot hide any chips behind their ties. The only pocket they have is a shirt pocket right over the left breast, usually for friendly genial blackjack players to slip a tip into (women do this in a motherly fashion). The Dealer, of

course, removes the tip from his shirt to be put into the general fund.

The Casino Manager must be very careful in choosing his executives, his Pit Bosses, Floorwalkers, and Laddermen. He will try to avoid picking "bleeders" or "sweaters." That is, executives who so hate to see the player win they may cheat the customer without the permission of the hotel, just out of sheer competitiveness.

One night the cast and crew of a film shooting in the nearby desert came into Las Vegas for a night on the town. The Director was a degenerate gambler with unlimited credit and a faulty understanding of the percentages. The Casino Manager welcomed him with open arms. Unfortunately the Director was accompanied by the Leading Lady of the film who had a profound belief in the powers of the zodiac.

The Director signed a marker for five grand worth of chips and started toward the nearest blackjack table, his favorite game. But the Leading Lady wouldn't let him play until they could find a dealer who was a Libra. She said the Director's sign, Taurus, demanded that on this particular day he would get lucky with a Libra.

So the two of them went down the rows of blackjack tables asking the Dealers what their birthdates were. Oddly enough, after canvassing all twenty tables they couldn't come up with a Libra Dealer. The law of averages said there had to be a least one, since there are only twelve signs of the zodiac.

What the Director and Leading Lady didn't understand was the character of the Las Vegas blackjack dealer. He is the perfect casino instrument. What the classic English butler is to English high society the Vegas dealer is to gambling society. They are exquisitely polite and coolly reserved. They know their places and are never familiar with players, but they also have their personal dignity.

So when the Leading Lady asked the Dealers for their birthdays, they took it as an affront. She was being presumptuous and so they either gave her a quiet smile and kept dealing or gave a false date. Finally the Leading Lady appealed to the Casino Manager for a Libra. He reassured her. The Dealers would take a break soon and a fresh crew would come on. Surely there would be a Libra among them. And then he inquired exactly what a Libra is. The Leading Lady explained that it was anybody born from September 23 to October 22.

Before the new crew came out the Casino Manager told one of them he was a Libra and born on the first of October. Prudently, just in case, he asked the Dealer what his birthday really was. The Dealer assured him he was born in March. The Leading Lady latched onto the lying Dealer and let the Director sit down to play. The Director had the first big winning night in his life. He won twenty grand on just that one shift. The Leading Lady was also delighted and bragged about her knowledge of the zodiac. This infuriated the Casino Manager who believed that only marked decks and second-carding could influence the percentages. It was an insult to everything he had built his life on that the signs of the zodiac could influence the games of chance. But he held his peace until the Leading Lady decreed that the Director was to quit while he was ahead by order of the signs of the zodiac.

Turning the whole thing into a joke in the hope that the Director would keep playing, the Casino Manager said to his Dealer, "Tell the Lady what your real birthday is."

At that moment the Director was putting five one-hundred-dollar chips in the Dealer's hand. The Leading Lady grabbed his hand to stop him.

The Casino Manager said, "Go ahead, tell her." His tone was full of contempt.

The Dealer took one look at the Leading Lady. He read her like a marked deck. "My birthday is the first of October," he said. And the Leading Lady released the Director's hand and let him tip the Dealer his $500. And then she led him firmly to bed, a twenty-grand winner by the power of the zodiac.

The Casino Manager has to know the real premium customer to whom he will give walking-away money. That is $100 or $200 to spend, not gamble, when the high roller is broke.

The Casino Manager has to keep track of every blackjack Dealer and dice Croupier and dice Boxman and how they win or lose at the tables they work.

The Casino Manager knows that a table must win approximately 20 percent of the drop. This can vary within a short space of time but if a Dealer is unlucky over a long period of time, he is guilty of cheating.

Now this is as good a time as any to explain how the casino operates. Customers buy chips with money or credit and the Dealer inserts this money into the slot in the table into a drop box locked underneath. That money is now called a "drop" and it represents the customers' collective bankroll. It is the money gambled against the casino. After every shift these boxes are removed from the table and counted in the Counting Room. A table should win 20 percent of the drop. This 20 percent is called a "hold." Out of this 20 percent the casino pays for entertainers, free food, beverages, etc. The percentage can vary from 18 percent to 22 percent but during the month it should never vary more than that.

HIGH SCORE
ONE
76

Every Casino Manager knows that the success of his casino is determined by the number of rooms in the hotel. For any new hotel to be profitable it must have at least 1,000 rooms. The Casino Manager has to explain delicately to the hotel manager that super-efficient room service hurts casino business. Lousy room service will drive the customer into the coffee shops and the restaurant and from there it's just a short step to the casino. The television sets in the rooms should not be of the most modern vintage, but should not be as bad as those in hospitals.

The Casino Manager has to keep an eye on the Junkets and Junket Master. He has to make sure that a Junket Master doesn't slip in fake players with fake IDs who will draw large amounts of cash on credit and walk out of the casino. Never to be heard from again, leaving their markers to gather dust.

The Casino Manager has to establish a chain of command. He has three Shift Bosses for each particular shift who are responsible to him. Shift Bosses have Pit Bosses. There's a Pit Boss for the blackjack pit where all the blackjack tables are, a Pit Boss for the dice pit, and one for baccarat.

Pit Bosses have Floormen who walk up and down behind the Dealers to make sure they stay honest. The baccarat table has a guy who sits in a very high

Kindergarten for degenerate slot machine gamblers.

chair so he can look down and keep an eye on everybody and he is called the Ladderman.

The only executive who works at a gaming table is the Boxman at craps. He sits at the center of the table, keeps an eye on the supply of chips to the Dealer, checks the plays. He also decides arguments about bets. He is also the guy who checks the dice to see if anybody has switched in strange ones. When dice go off the table he always takes a look at them before they go back into play.

The dice of a casino are marked with a special code that only a Boxman can read so that strange dice cannot be switched.

Some gamblers have trained themselves to control the dice even when they are rolling them out. The only way to prevent this is to require that the dice be bounced off the other end of the table. Also, no Boxman allows a Dealer to take chips directly from a player's hand because the higher-denomination chips could be switched from house to player.

Like the infantryman in combat, the Dealer faces the gambling world head to head. He sells chips to customers, pays off their victories, collects their losses, deals the cards, puts up with bad jokes, sour tempers, obnoxious winners, and sore losers. Since the major part of his income depends on tips, he roots for the customers. He will be sympathetic to the loser. He will congratulate the winner on his luck. And sometimes he helps.

Estimates vary but, counting tips, a Dealer easily makes $500 a week. (Like true gamblers seeking an "Edge," Dealers claim that their tips are tax-free because they are not rendering a service.)

He gets twenty minutes off every hour and when he leaves his post he wishes all the players good luck, washes his hands high in the air to show he is not concealing chips, and goes to the Dealers' rest room where, more than likely, he will play poker with other Dealers to pass the twenty minutes.

The Casino Manager has to assign a Dealer to the game that suits his personality. The hardest game to deal is craps. The Dealers working the crap table should be tall with long reaches. They have to handle bets over vast expanses of green felt. They also should be extraverts. Craps is an extraverted game. Players chat with each other, cheer each other on. It becomes a community enterprise.

The Dealers at the crap table root for the players, again since their tips depend on winners, not losers. The action at a crap table can become very hectic, very complicated.

Dealers are trained to encourage bets that have a high casino advantage. The "hard ways," the "field bets," the one-

ELECTRONIC 21

roll "11s," the one-roll craps, all with a house percentage that goes up to a killer 17 percent to 18 percent.

The Stickman at the crap table should be a Mary Poppins optimist, delight in his voice when he calls out a winner. His overwhelming confidence for a shooter coming up with an 11 encourages everybody to get on it despite its 18 percent disadvantage. A good Stickman never calls out "seven, loser" but rather "seven, line away." The word *lose* is not in his vocabulary. The Boxman usually remains impassive. He keeps an eye on everybody.

The Dealers and the Stickmen are encouraged to root for the gambler against the house, but not always.

In one of the biggest hotels on the Strip, the casino crap tables got hot for the players. Against all the odds week after week, the players beat the house. The casino was giving out thousands of dollars the way Rockefeller handed out dimes. At the end of the first month, the casino kept the closest possible check on all crap table personnel. At the end of the second month, it had all the dice tested by special laboratories and all tables scanned for magnets. At the end of the third month it called on the Nevada Gaming Commission for help. But nobody could find anything wrong. At a billion-to-one odds, the casino was losing a fortune. There was no other explanation except luck. Except, maybe, a master crook had found a way to beat the system and reduce Las Vegas casinos to whimpering bust-out slot machine joints. All the casino owner could do was wait.

At the end of the third month the plague ended. The crap tables returned to their winning percentages and the casino owners gave up their plans of suicide. But they live in the constant fear that it could happen again.

A blackjack Dealer is more reserved and gentlemanly. He never speaks unless spoken to. He gets more abuse than any other Dealer because he is more directly an opponent to the player. In blackjack you are playing against the Dealer's cards or so it seems and if the Dealer gets lucky, the losing players often feel a resentment against him personally. This makes the Dealer very wary. What also makes the Dealer at blackjack very wary is the knowledge that he is a marked man. Behind him stand the Floorwalker, the Pit Boss, the Shift Boss, the Casino Manager, all of whom can fire him on a mere suspicion or if he gets too unlucky against all the laws of percentage.

One retired blackjack Dealer told me that if you don't get greedy and you had a trustworthy confederate "outside" you could clear twenty grand a year without any chance of getting caught. The only trouble with the theory, he says, is nobody can stop himself from getting greedy.

Lowest on the scale of employees are the Shills. They are people gambling at the gaming tables with the casino's money to create an impression of activity. Today they are used mostly at baccarat tables. They are also called "starters." You can always spot them at the baccarat table because they bet the table minimum and always bet against the bank unless they have the bank in their hands.

There are many stories about Shills. Remember, a Shill is just a fake player employed by the casino to fill up the table. He plays with casino money. When he wins, it's the casino money. When he loses, it's the casino money. He draws maybe $150 a week salary, win or lose. Some Shills have lucky streaks that of course avail them nothing. They may win for weeks and weeks and the money just goes back to the casino. So inevitably they risk their salaries at another casino and almost invariably lose. Other Shills may invariably lose. Thinking they are due to win just by the law of averages, they also invest their own money at another casino. They too invariably lose. All this is quite ordinary.

But what can cause trouble is that sometimes a Real Big player decides a certain Shill is lucky and will bet with that Shill when she has the bank in baccarat. There is nothing more infuriating to a casino manager than to see his house beat by a big player riding on a Shill's luck. And sometimes a Shill will get a bad reputation for being lucky and have trouble finding casino work.

A classic case is the story of a young beautiful girl who came to Vegas and got a job as a baccarat Shill in one of the finest hotels. The very fact that she was beautiful made players bet with her when she got the bank. And she was very lucky. The baccarat table regulars were cleaning up. The Casino Boss was infuriated. He took an interest in her and learned that she was a straight arrow. That she didn't turn tricks and didn't even have a boyfriend. The Casino Manager decided that the reason she was lucky was that she was a virgin. So he made the decision that if she remained a virgin he would fire her. If she turned a trick he would keep her on. He so told one of the Laddermen bossing the baccarat pit.

But how to get this straight-arrow girl to agree to give up her virginity? The Ladderman fixed her up with big players who would be thousand-dollar tricks. The girl refused. And remained lucky. A Pit Boss persuaded one of the top show biz stars to take a shot at her. No dice. She stood fast. And lucky. Finally the casino boss fired her and passed the word around town. The girl left Vegas. A customer returned a month afterward and asked why his favorite Shill was gone. The Casino Manager told him "bad vibes." Virtue is its own reward.

Casinos make no secret of the Shills. They know that gamblers want a physical presence with them when they gamble at the table. On one of my trips to Vegas I sat down at a baccarat table for my very first shot at that game. There was a quiet dignified gentleman sitting in one of the seats. Suddenly, a much better dressed, much more imposing-looking man tapped him on the shoulder. The player got up and the other man took his place. I immediately weaved a fantasy. The man sitting down was a high-rolling gambler who had paid the other man to hold his place at the table. I didn't know it was just one Shill replacing another Shill.

All this is the Casino Manager's domain. He also has to keep track of the gambling equipment, the roulette wheels, the decks of cards that are used, dice that are used. All equipment is coded and numbered serially. All precautions have to be taken to prevent counterfeits from being switched into the game.

A Casino Manager must also know the eccentricities of slot machine players. He must know that for some reason dime machines are not popular. People go from a 5¢ machine to a 25¢ machine. My own personal theory is that the gambling animal is basically primitive. He just can't believe that the small, thin dime can be worth more than the heavier, wider nickel.

The Casino Manager must also know that slot machines and to some extent roulette have the primary function of keeping wives and girlfriends out of the hair of their men who are doing some serious gambling at crap tables, baccarat, and blackjack.

The Casino Manager understands that keno is the five-and-dime store variety of gambling indulged in only by the very poorest of gamblers looking for a $25,000 prize with a 60¢ ticket. Despite the fact that keno gives the casino its greatest "Edge," it provides the smallest flow of revenue.

Casino Managers have sought to raise the keno prize to $100,000 but the Nevada Gaming Commission does not want gamblers to go up against the 20 percent "Edge."

The Casino Manager is also responsible for the Cashier's Cage holding a million dollars in cash and chips. Chips in the casino are counted at the end of each shift, three times every twenty-four hours, table by table, and also in the Cashier's Cage. This is to prevent counterfeit chips from being run in on a large scale. Also the Pit Bosses and the Floormen always keep track of the high-denomination chips at their pit tables.

The Casino Manager through his Shift Boss and Pit Boss also has to handle Claim Agents. These are gamblers who are very adept at raising a dispute over a bet. The famous Nick the Greek was a great Claim Agent. Casino Managers had to tread a fine line, allowing enough of Nick's claims to keep their percentage, allowing enough of his claims so that he would keep playing at their particular casinos. After all, Nick the Greek was famous not only for being the biggest gambler of his time, but also more important, the biggest *loser* of his time. He was, as far as I can judge, the classic degenerate gambler.

The Casino Manager knows that the casino has to win its money three times. The first time at the tables, the second time from the employees who steal it, and then finally when they have to collect the markers. And what happens is that in the heat of gambling, with the religious instinct of the true believer in the return of Jesus Christ, knowing your luck will turn, you sign markers. In no time at all you have lost 20 to 50 grand. And you just came to town to have a good time and drop a thousand at the tables.

Under the present-day management of conglomerates Casino Managers are losing some of their power. For instance a Casino Manager doesn't mind giving out a million dollars' worth of credit and losing $200,000 of it in bad collections. He figures he's $800,000 to the good. The more conservative businessmen who are now coming into power in Vegas are horrified. They think they are giving that $200,000 away. They would rather give $500,000 in credit and be able to collect $480,000 and only lose $20,000 in bad collections. It's really a question of Western thinking against Eastern thinking. Never the twain shall meet.

Casino Managers brought up in the tradition of the gambling West never worry too much about a guy not paying his markers as long as he loses plenty of cash up front. After all, they have not given the man real cash to walk away with, they have merely given him chips to gamble with. Chips that come right back into the Cashier's Cage.

The Casino Manager also has to worry about his Collectors. He must constantly remind them that when they collect markers the aim is to keep the losers as customers even if they have to make a deal in which they settle for less than the face amount of the markers.

He instructs the Collectors never to contact the customer at his home, that the Collector should function also as a public relations representative, to be charming and always make any sort of arrangement to keep the customer happy even if he cannot pay his markers. A customer who is broke is

Vegas is so square that they still use Victorian words like screw.

HAPPINESS IS
A GOOD SCREW

still, by his earning power, valuable in the future. There are, of course, some rascals perfectly able to pay who feel that since gambling debts are not legally collectible, they simply will not pay. Collectors will then get tougher. Of course, no threats, nothing illegal, but they are allowed to be a little shrewish, to use a delicate word. For instance, they can institute suit against a well-known businessman for collection of debts even though they know the suit will fail. There will be enough publicity to make the businessman famous as a reckless gambler and, therefore, not a really trustworthy businessman.

Beyond all this stand the IRS and the Nevada Gaming Commission. Since even the gross tax is not collected on markers, if they are not paid, the Nevada Gaming Commission is very strict about the hotel's making a legitimate effort to collect markers. This is the same Gaming Commission that refuses to make gambling a legally collectible debt. This may seem a contradiction, but it is really sound thinking. Legalization of gambling debts in Nevada would be disastrous for the gaming industry. The papers would be filled with stories of businessmen losing their businesses; farmers losing their farms; blue-collar workers getting their salaries attached. Las Vegas would turn into dust and as ghostlike as the old mining towns. But on the other hand the Gaming Commission has to

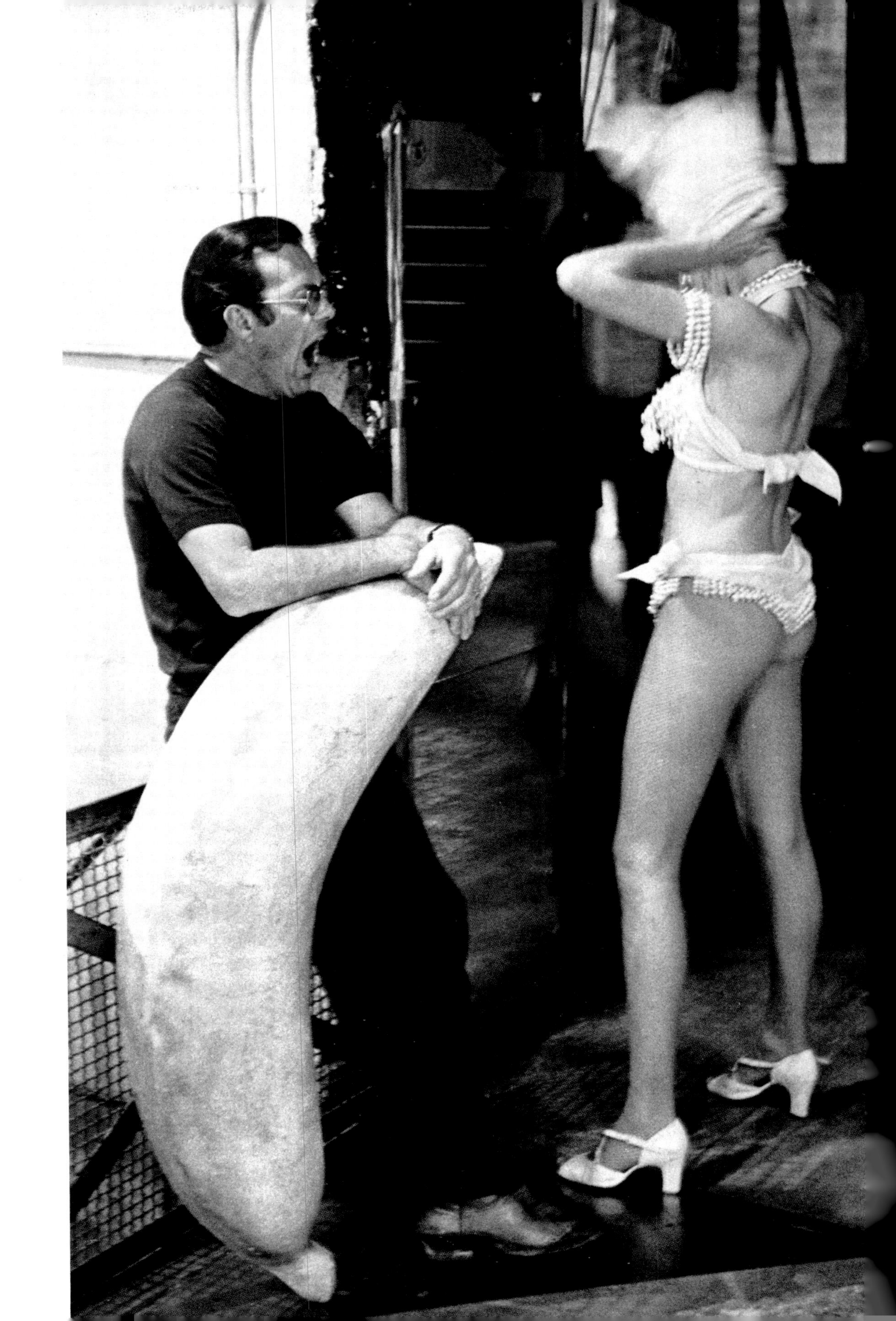

be suspicious when the hotel is less than enthusiastic about collecting its markers. Are private deals being made between the casino and the debtor?

For instance, if a big gambler owes $100,000 in markers, will he slip the Casino Manager 20 grand to tear them up? There have been rumored cases of Casino Managers actually being in cahoots with gamblers to extend them big credit for kickbacks. The more frequent of these cases are famous entertainers who come to work in Vegas for fabulous salaries and lose their money at the tables. In former years the management merely deducted losses from such an entertainer's salary. The law has been changed and hotels can no longer do this. The salary must be paid to the entertainer. But then the hotel is in a dilemma. If it has a star attraction who draws millions of dollars in gamblers' money and the entertainer loses a couple of hundred grand, how can it insist on payment? The entertainer who loses $200,000 gambling, non-tax deductible, must earn $600,000 to pay that $200,000 debt. As an ordinary sensitive human being he must resent this. As a hardheaded businessman he tells the hotel "tear up my markers or I don't entertain." Business is business. A way is found to tear up the markers. And this is not to imply that anything illegal is done. The hotel does attempt to collect; the entertainer refuses to pay. By law nothing can be done. The debt is not a legally collectible debt.

The Casino Manager must also know that speed is an important factor in all gambling games, especially in keno. The more turnover, the more games played, the more chance the casino has of becoming a winner. The percentage of "Edge" grinds the player out.

If the casinos wanted to cheat, here's how they could do it.

At the dice table it would be simple enough. They could just run in loaded or angled dice. A lot of this was done in the gambling hells of England in the 1700s and onward. Usually late at night or in the early morning hours when the dupes were drunk. Also the bets at the crap table fly fast and furious. When you bet all the numbers they can shortchange you on your winning odds. Also they could call out the wrong number of the dice, call a seven out and scoop up the dice.

At roulette they can really kill you. There are ways to rig the wheel with concealed electronic magnets and a ball with a steel core. By pressing buttons under the table the Dealer can affect the roll of the ball. But this would be suicide in a place like Vegas.

More likely is the highly skilled Croupier who can influence where the ball will land by spinning the wheel at a certain speed and throwing the ball a certain way. This method is not foolproof and can only control the sections where the ball will land, but the Croupier can increase the house advantage from 5 percent to 15 percent. (It's not nice to be mean to a Croupier.) A favorite trick is to spin the wheel very slowly so that the ball will just plunk into the nearest pocket. Make sure you get a fast spin. There's no way you can check the size and weight of the ball, which are also important.

The house can beat you at blackjack by simply putting in a mechanic against you. That is, a man who can deal cards so skillfully that he can stick an Ace of Spades in your eye and you'll never see it. He can stack the decks in sequences to make you lose. If the deck is in his hands and not in a shoe he can "second card" you to death. That is, he can tell if there is a good card for his blackjack hand on top of the deck and save it for himself by dealing the players the card underneath that top card. It is impossible to see him do this. He is too fast. But if you listen closely you can hear the hiss or tick of the second card sliding out from underneath the top card. The house could also drug you, make you drunk, roll you, blackmail you, and even knock you off. But to what purpose? You, the player, are like a husband who only carries 2 grand worth of life insurance. You are worth more alive, working, earning money every year to lose every year. Which is why if you owe them a lot of money they will work something out. One of the biggest misconceptions about gambling is that bookmakers and casino creditors get angry and break bust-out gamblers' legs. I have known a bookmaker to pay a surgeon's fee for a bust-out client who owed him thousands in markers. Not from a heart of gold but to protect his property. The guy owed, but he still gambled his paycheck every week. If he lost he lost cash. If he won, the bookie just took it off his markers at 50 percent. A degenerate gambler is regarded as a fine bit of rent-yielding property. You take care of him. And most of all there are the Nevada Gaming Commission investigators ready to jump in and suspend the casino license if there is any dirty work.

So don't worry when you go to Vegas. You will get a fair shake and it is maybe the only place you will get a fair and square deal. In Europe your fellow player, a German countess and Italian marchesa, will try to steal your roulette bet. The Croupiers may spit on you figuratively if you protest their decision. In Vegas such things don't happen. Nobody tries to steal your bet in roulette because every player has his own color of chips. And the Croupiers don't spit on you (unless you spit on them first) because you both speak the

same language and also because in Vegas the player in a dispute always gets the first decision, the benefit of the doubt. The Pit Boss will merely say "pay the player." However, the second time you dispute a call you could have some trouble.

But the big danger in Vegas is crooked players or "crossroaders," ripping off the casino and in the process hurting a few innocent bystanders plus getting the casino in trouble with the law. (One Casino Manager stays up nights unable to sleep because "there are ten million guys out there trying to steal from me.") If a player sneaks a loaded pair of dice onto the crap table and the Gaming Commission finds them in play, the casino gets its license suspended. Even though it is a victim, the casino is responsible.

At roulette the crooked customer doesn't have much chance to cheat. He can slip in a magnetized ball but the Croupier periodically checks the ball against a bit of metal embedded in the table for just that purpose. He can also try to get into the equipment room and fix a wheel by laying thin lead sheets in the pockets of certain numbers making them harder to win because the ball has less space to fit into. Then bet all the other numbers.

A bit of petty larceny in roulette is pretending to count your chips when the number has hit and slipping another chip on the pile.

For scientists there is an intriguing possibility. Red and black paint differ in their chemical properties and reactions. Black paint tends to make the wooden fibers of the slot hard, making the ball bounce out. Therefore red is the better color to play. The red paint eats into the wooden fibers of the slot thus making the floor of the red pockets less resilient so that instead of jumping out the ball will stick. This is not a proven theory because the percentage is so small and tests have not been made to prove it out. I think the fact is that you remember red coming up more often simply because it is the more vivid color.

There is a legitimate beating of the casino when the casino is careless with its equipment. A crack in the wooden floor of the wheel underneath the middle slot can give the player the "Edge" if he observes the wheel long enough. So can the loosening of slots. Teams of players keeping track of the performance of certain wheels have made big scores in Europe and Vegas but the house catches on and retires the wheel or simply disguises it. Generally speaking even these defects do not overcome the house percentage of 5 plus. If you are looking to cheat the house or beat it legitimately, forget about roulette. It's basically a sucker's game. In fact, early on in its American career, to make the public forget the

Showgirls.

tough odds they had to beat, with the extra 00 slots, they had what was called mouse roulette in which instead of a ball a mouse was put on the spinning wheel and whatever slot it hid in was the winning number. Which shows gambling wizards will try anything.

Casinos make the most money with slot machines, a nickel, a dime, a quarter, or a dollar at a time. They invent newer and flashier machines with all kinds of symbols to show jackpots. Different-colored fruits and bars and other motifs delight the eye as they whirl through the window of the slot machine. It is surely an infantile pleasure, the closest you can get to childhood. But though they make the most money, to casinos they also pose the gravest security problem.

For some time players could beat the machines legitimately with what is called the "rhythm method." Rhythm players learned how to control the spins of internal wheels by pulling the handle a split second after the wheels came to rest from the previous play. This threw the internal controlling mechanism out of whack. Finally this was eliminated by the invention of a new controlling gadget but there is no way to protect a slot machine from crooked operators except by constant surveillance of the slot layouts.

Another scam on slot machines is to insert a piece of wire or a "shim" into a small opening in front of the machine to hold the reels in place. If you are really ambitious you can use a small battery-operated drill and punch a hole into the slot machine and then insert a wire. If you are a primitive you can keep banging the handle to release the lock. If you're a clever mechanic fixing one of the machines you can put an ice cube between the fly wheels so that it will control the wheels as the ice cube melts.

It is estimated that there are more than 60,000 slot machines in Nevada and nearly 3,000 gaming tables. You can get a slot machine to bring home with you. A used beat-up one will cost you around $150. The problem is its maintenance.

Hustlers buy slot machines to take apart and study for any weak spots. They develop small drills with which they can noiselessly bore into the side of the slot machine and empty out the cash. Remember, slot machines are in all the retail stores, lunch counters, etc. Remember that slot machines are crammed into every available corner of the casino. It is tough to spot these drillers but casinos have cops in plain clothes wandering around.

Another penny ante trick is using cheap foreign coins, especially Mexican, to put into the machines.

Wardrobe mistresses.

But perhaps the most interesting method is the use of magnets. You can control the spinning of the wheels in a slot machine with powerful magnets. In one case a married couple made a career ripping off the slot machines pressurally. The man would play a machine while the woman would stand behind him. When they were taken into custody the woman's purse was found to contain a seventy-five pound magnet, powerful enough to make the machine stand up and beg. A police officer just out of amused curiosity asked the tiny woman how she could carry that seventy-five-pound magnet around all day. She gave him a sweet smile and said, "Practice."

The stopping of slot machine stealing is merely a matter of hiring enough people, honest people, to keep an eye on the machines.

The mechanic who services the machines sets the return rate (machines are regulated to give a certain percentage of payoff). That is, a machine can be set so that you can play for an average of ten minutes to lose a dollar. The mechanic has a key to the machines worth his weight in gold but one bad move on his part and he is out of a job forever, and remember it is a well-paying job.

The most truly draining and dangerous of operations for the casino, the greatest threat to its sacred "bankroll," is blackjack. And the threat is double-pronged. It is the easiest game for players and dealers to steal from the house. It is also the only casino game in which, believe it or not, the player can work a percentage or edge against the house. In other words it is the only casino game in which it is mathematically possible for the player to win.

Cheating at blackjack is almost invariably done by the player or customer, not the casino. It is nearly always done with the help of an employee of the casino, usually the Dealer. There have been cases in which the Dealer has also enlisted the help of the Floorwalker and Pit Boss. This is called "dumping out."

Just a simple old-fashioned American free enterprise system of partnership. The blackjack Dealer goes "halfies" with a player who is also a friend of his. A crossroader. They have a set of signals by which the Dealer can inform the player what the Dealer's hole card is. Once the player knows the Dealer's hole card the percentage immediately switches over to the player's hand. (Remember the casino advantage is that the customer must play his hand first and risk going "bust.") If the Dealer has a ten, a seven, or eight or nine up, the computer percentage says the player with less than seventeen has to hit even if he takes a chance of busting. If the Dealer has anything from a deuce to six up and the player has a hand that can bust, then the percentage is that the player must stand and wait for the Dealer to, he hopes, bust. Well, if the Dealer has a good card up but signals the player that he has a hand that can bust, for example a ten up but a deuce to six in the hole, the player can stand on his own bustable hand and let the Dealer go bust. If you can get this arrangement with a Dealer it's better than a federal license to deal heroin.

A Dealer can signal to his confederate in many ways. Remember the Casino Bosses were not born yesterday. Many casino executives were former Dealers who hustled a little. They know the score. So a Dealer is not allowed to look at his hole card unless he has a ten-point or an ace as his face-up card. The casinos have TV monitors on the Dealer, a Floorman walking up and down behind, a Pit Boss making checks. The Shift Boss keeps his fingers in the pie. Cheating is made difficult. So signals have to be very subtle or the Dealer is out of work. But at least his punishment is not as severe as it used to be in the early days when a cheating Dealer had a good chance of having all his fingers broken. Today he gets fired and has a tough time getting another job in the gaming industry.

But sometimes a whole gang gets together to make a really big score. The Dealer has to be in on it, of course. This involves getting a card shoe and decks of cards that duplicate the casino's. The shoe is then prepared with stacked decks in certain sequences. The six members of the conspiracy, usually five men and one woman, fully occupy the slots of a blackjack table. Another confederate starts a fight at the next table to divert the attention of the Pit Boss and Floorwalker. At that moment the woman confederate whips the prepared shoe out of her huge purse and puts it on the table. With the same motion she snatches the casino shoe and puts it in her purse. The Dealer, who is in on it, looks off into the distance. When the fight at the next table has been quieted and order restored, everybody gets back to business. The six crossroaders at the table make big bets and win and get paid off by the Dealer under the now watchful but unsuspecting eyes of the Floorwalker and Pit Boss. By the time the shoe runs out of cards the conspirators at the table have maybe pocketed a hundred grand. Midway through this operation the woman has left the table with the incriminating shoe in her purse so that even if the casino operators catch on (by this time they have) there is no evidence against the players at the table.

Another trick is to plant a very tiny mirror inside the card shoe so that it reflects the next card coming out. Only someone looking for it could notice it and the Dealer who, of course, must be a party to this tampering with equipment positions the shoe so that only his confederate can read the mirror. Some good scores have been made with this trick but it is dangerous because the mirror can be found by a Floorwalker or Pit Boss and it becomes legal evidence of a crime.

And then there is of course the straight-out stealing by using sleight of hand. Some Dealers wear the equivalent of the old-time woman's bloomers with the elastic fitting snugly against their thighs. They would use this as a drop by slipping a hundred-dollar chip inside their trousers. This was called a "submarine." Also a Croupier was found with a specially made thick wristwatch into which he could slip a high-value chip where the works should be. Of course he never knew what the hell time it was. Then there was the specially built "stack" of $5 chips that looked like five chips. It was actually one hollow chip with a spring contraption. The Dealer could press it down on the hundred-dollar chips which it would enclose, then pass it on to a confederate on the other side of the blackjack table to make change. So what looked like a stack of five-dollar chips worth $25 was actually a hollow with four one-hundred-dollar chips inside it.

It has now been proved by computer that blackjack is the only casino game at which the player can legitimately beat the house.

Scientists at the Atomic Energy Laboratory in Los Alamos, New Mexico, used idle computers. In the Army's proving ground in Maryland a man named Bob Bamford built an electronic black box and the computer told him when to take a hit or not. He claimed it gave him a 5 percent advantage. He did win some hundreds of dollars but then was thrown out of the casinos. Yes, sad but true. Vegas casinos do throw out successful "count-downers," despite the fact that they are perfectly legal. Then Edward Thorpe's book on beating the Dealer based on computer analysis seemed to be successful. It made the casinos change their blackjack rules, temporarily.

> SPECIAL NOTE: Except for the few card-counters who can count down from a shoe, all this stuff means nothing because if anyone does figure out how to beat the Dealer the rules will be changed or the cards reshuffled after each hand.

Dealing blackjack, casinos will have to install more and more electronic devices and computers to protect themselves. Closed TV circuits are already used for surveillance on gaming tables. Company owners are more and more aware of computer and radio communications devices.

WOMEN OF LAS VEGAS

ALAD

FEDERAL RESERVE NOTE
B
THE UNITED STATES OF AMERICA
ONE THOUSAND DOLLARS
1000

Las Vegas has more beautiful women than any town its size in the world. It may have as many beautiful women as any city in the world no matter what its size. The reason for this is quite simple and only superficially cynical: MONEY and beautiful women zing together like two magnets. Especially in Vegas.

The girls and women come from all over the United States and, indeed, from all over the world. They come in many ways and for many reasons. It is American folklore that the prettiest girl in every small town or city escapes to Hollywood seeking fame and fortune. If she misses Las Vegas in her rush to movie stardom, the odds are that, sadder and wiser, she will hit Las Vegas on her way home. Reluctant to return to friends and family defeated, she will quite likely remain in Vegas to make her fortune in ways that do not require extraordinary talents.

This sounds like a put-down of such women. It is not meant to be. In our civilization a woman's beauty is a capital asset. With so many other roads barred to her, a beautiful woman must use her body, her face, her charm as a means to riches. Women are encouraged to do so by men. They are conditioned to do so by our social system. It is not a happy solution for many women, but it beats working nine to five.

Many of the thousands whose dreams crash in Hollywood come to Vegas and become high-class call girls. Others become "soft" hustlers. A soft hustler, ideally, is one who makes a permanent relationship with men for one-week periods until she has a stable of twenty men who never give her cash for each sexual bout but who buy her presents and give her gambling money and sometimes marriage.

Many women are attracted to Vegas because of the hotels' need for beautiful girls in their showrooms. The Vegas spectaculars feature statuesque nudes who are chosen for their looks. They need not be skilled dancers. The real dancing is done by still another group of girls who are really talented, many superbly trained and with great pride in their art. All these girls work very hard and are as virtuous as the girl next door, which means of course that most of them are no longer virgin dummies. Many of them are married to Dealers and musicians and you would be surprised at the number of those lust-inspiring beauties who have three or four kids. It would be a lie to say that none of them is available, to a charming and generous high-roller, but fewer are than one might think.

Then there are the cocktail waitresses. Pretty girls can earn enormous tips and in earlier days they were expected to become bedmates to favored gamblers if a Pit Boss gave them the word.

She cheers up the losers. A spectacular Las Vegas show costs more than a Broadway musical. The casinos don't actually make money on the shows. You must walk through the casino to get to the show and back through the casino on your way out. The idea is to draw you to the gambling tables.

Then there are the Shills, the girls employed to fill up the baccarat table when business is slow and play with house money. Some of these girls are available, some are not. If they are dressed provocatively and smile a lot you can usually arrange something with the local Pit Boss, provided you are a substantial "player."

Another source of supply is the Weekend Call Girl. These modern young ladies work all week at "respectable" jobs in towns like Los Angeles and Salt Lake City, Utah. They may be secretaries, manicurists, dental technicians, etc. Maybe it started when they went to Vegas for a weekend of fun and shows with a boyfriend or even a girlfriend. The Vegas gambling executives, Pit Bosses and Shift Bosses, have an eagle eye for such girls. They "chat them up," "put them into a show" (that is give them a free meal and seat to see a show), and then give the girls their business cards and tell them to call whenever they're in town and they need something. On a later solo trip the girls will usually be fixed up for a date with a hotshot gambler. This is all free will, no white slavery involved. What happens is that the girl has a great time with a garment center guy from New York or a semimillionaire from Texas. They have dinner together, he takes her to the best shows, he gives her money to gamble. (No Vegas gentleman lets a lady gamble with her own money.) At the end of the evening unless the guy is a real creep or completely degenerate gambler they naturally go to bed and spend the weekend together. On Monday morning the girl flies back to Los Angeles or Salt Lake City all plus: If she won gambling she has a month's wages stashed. If she lost, the non-creep gives her a parting gift of cash. She has had a pleasant, exciting weekend. She has spent it in the company of an interesting man. Usually an older man, it is true, perhaps a little fatter and balder than she would have liked, but still many of them are interesting. Back in her home town she again picks up the thread of a bourgeois life in which everybody thinks she is a "nice" girl and her local swain gives her flowers, respect, and an offer of marriage. It is an ideal situation. She can have it both ways. Few women, and fewer men, for that matter, can resist such temptation. If the girl is really a charmer the gambling executive will put in a call to her hometown when special situations arise, such as a big gambling multimillionaire oilman from Oklahoma coming into Vegas and needing a dinner date for the weekend.

There is never any coercion for the girl to go to bed. If she really doesn't like the guy she thanks him for a lovely evening and goes alone to her room. But given the circumstances it would have to be an extremely disagreeable man for her not to be charmed by him.

Her final destiny may go many ways. She can, finally, tire of the high life in Vegas and stay in her hometown, marry one of the local businessmen, and live the life of a wife and mother. She can move to Vegas permanently and become a high-class call girl exclusively. Or work there in an office. Or even become a Dealer, a degenerate gambler, or showgirl.

If she is really beautiful, acquires a reputation for being charming (*charming* here means simple sweetness, an easygoing nature, and a willingness to hang around while the man gambles and never having a headache when the man wants sex at any hour), and is discreet, she makes it to an exclusive list kept by hotel owners. When she is on one of those lists her future career is assured and she is completely protected from the obtuse and nondiscriminating majesty of the law.

A new big source of supply is the adventurous girlhood of America no longer resigned to the dull fate of marriage, motherhood, and wifedom who are out to sow their wild oats and have some fun. These become the ordinary run-of-the-mill prostitutes and call girls. They have to learn the rules of Vegas. No pimps. No blackmail. No clipping of wallets. If they do not observe these rules their careers will be cut short by the law. Remember the money they may be stealing belongs to the gambling casinos and is just temporarily being held by the John. At least this is the working attitude of the gaming establishment. Larcenous girls are really stealing casino money.

It is difficult to write about women who sell the act of sex for cash. On the one hand the moralists get terribly angry. On the other hand the women's liberation movements get terribly indignant. In the hope of placating both, here are three true stories about typical call girls in Vegas. Two in which the girl comes to a bad end, the other in which the girl triumphs over a male-supremacy society that has forced her into sexual bondage.

While writing these stories I find it difficult to use all the terms which seem to be the accepted definitions of our society. We label women who transact an act of sex for cash by what seems, in this day and age, cruel names. The words, whore, prostitute, call girl, hooker, hustler seem a bit unfair in a capitalistic society in which our most respected citizens perform far more dubious acts to make money. The Vegas term *working girl* I find a bit snobbish. I have tried to think of a new word but without success.

THE NURSE

Janet is a sweet twenty-four-year-old girl who worked as a nurse in a Vegas hospital. Somewhere along the way she developed a taste for gambling. But

she also had a very strong vocation for nursing. She also had a very strong sexual drive. She also had a Puritan conditioning. So, therefore, she was, emotionally, in a lot of trouble.

Janet had a good body, short-cropped golden hair, and a virginally wholesome face. But her great asset was her sweet good nature. One night a big-time degenerate gambler suffered a swift heart attack at a hot crap table. Protesting violently he was dragged to Janet's hospital where she became his nurse. A friendship developed and when the patient was discharged he gave Janet a handsome gift plus an offer for her to nurse him while he recuperated in the sunny climes of the Caribbean. Janet quit her job and went with him. The gambler recovered and became her lover when his doctor gave him the okay. As a percentage gambler he felt secure with her. If things went wrong while they were in the sack she knew what steps to take. She handled his medication. While he gambled she checked his pulse periodically and watched for any physical signs of a coming attack. She was a great nurse, great in the sack, and a sweet non-nagging gambling companion. The degenerate gambler had found the girl of his dreams.

Unfortunately out of an excess of guilt the gambler returned home to spend some time with his wife and children and to attend to his thriving business in meat packing. While living the sedentary careful life of a dutiful husband, father, and entrepreneur, he had a fatal heart attack. Possibly the presence of the Nurse might have rescued him from death. The ambulance team got to his home too late.

Janet was so overcome by guilt and remorse she returned to nursing at the Vegas hospital. She was such a fine dedicated nurse that she had no trouble getting back her old job in the intensive care unit.

Her deceased gambler friend had proclaimed her virtues far and wide. On her next night off when she went gambling at her favorite casinos the Pit Bosses couldn't do enough for her. They arranged for her to attend all the shows free, all her food and drinks were on the house. Her visiting friends and relatives were comped RFB (Room, Food, and Beverages). She had become the darling of the gambling world. She was known as a sweet, non-ball-breaking broad who was always cheerful, never scammed, never tried to hustle a male gambling companion, not greedy for money really, enthusiastically willing in the sack, and in a pinch qualified to rescue guys from fatal heart attacks at gambling tables. In short, a gambler's ideal weekend mistress. There was only one time in her history when she became angry. A crazily superstitious degenerate gambler asked her to wear her nurse uniform and cap at the crap table. She spit in his eye and the Pit Boss had the guy's leg broken.

Janet, or as she came to be known almost exclusively, the Nurse, was soon a legend in the town. She was that rare type of woman, rare at any rate in Vegas, who loved a loser perhaps more than a winner. Some of her cases became famous stories in Vegas.

There was the garment center manufacturer who came to Vegas to forget his troubles. His business was going bankrupt (don't ask where he got the money to gamble, desperate men always do), his wife was divorcing him and had taken possession of his house on Long Island plus his new Cadillac. His daughter had run away with a black homosexual, his son was a right-wing patriotic American who had volunteered to fight in Vietnam. With the perverse logic of the true degenerate gambler he figured God was testing his faith, saving a great reward for him. That reward, he was certain, was a brilliant coup at the crap table. He would hold the dice for an hour and run off a hundred numbers. He would win enough money to stave off his firm's bankruptcy, buy a new house on Long Island, win a young wife, and start a new family of bright children. (Perhaps he was not a degenerate gambler, but just an ordinary American optimist.)

Anyway he came to Vegas with a good-sized bankroll. Held the dice for three seconds. He sevened out without even throwing a number, much less a pass. He tried baccarat out of desperation and got caught in the baccarat trap. He zigged when he should have zagged, that is he bet banker when he should have bet player and then switched when the shoe switched. He did not have one winning bet. He messed around with blackjack and busted every hand for a whole shoe. Finally in desperation he gambled his last chips at roulette. Determined to be a winner at least once, he covered 34 numbers out of the total of 38 (counting the green 0 and 00). Unbelievably the ball plunked into the hole of one of the four numbers he left uncovered.

The shattered degenerate gambler wailed aloud. He was another Job. Why was God doing this to him? Nobody could be so unlucky.

His Host took pity on him, afraid he might do something terrible. An urgent call was sent out for the Nurse. The degenerate gambler sneered at the thought that a lousy hooker could solve his problems, that the age-old familiar act of sex with a paid instrument could remove the death wound to his soul. Had not even God deserted him? The Host sent the degenerate gambler up to his room to await the arrival of the Nurse. Then the Host put in a call to room service and had champagne and the best dinner sent to the room plus a smuggled box of rich Havana cigars hoarded only for the top gamblers.

The Nurse entered the room. She cradled the poor degenerate gambler's head. She listened to his many tales of woe. She wept for him. She put him in the bathtub and bathed him from head to foot. From her purse she took bottles of special oils and perfumes and anointed him. She had him lie back on the bed and relax and then used all her professional knowledge of the human anatomy to bring him pleasure. Then they ate the dinner and drank the champagne. She lit his cigar and took puffs on it with him. He was a little happier, a little more relaxed. He told her he had no money. She told him she had a thousand-dollar line of credit at the casino that was at his disposal. He couldn't believe it. A hotel hooker was giving him money to gamble. Why? Why? Because, the Nurse told him, he had a beautiful sensitive face. And because he made her so happy. The gambler still didn't believe her and said okay he would gamble her thousand dollars. At first he was suspicious that the hotel was actually supplying her the money to give him but on reflection he knew this was impossible. No casino gives away a grand to enable a sucker to win his money back.

They gambled. His luck turned. He won five thousand dollars. They went back to the room. The gambler found himself falling in love with this beautiful sweet girl who, between bouts of sex, listened to all his troubles with such sympathy that tears sprang to her lovely blue eyes. Finally, exhausted he fell into a deep sleep. When he awoke in the morning he was surprised to find the Nurse still there and the five grand still in his pockets. Also on the night table was a little present she had bought him from the hotel gift shop. A lucky charm of a rattlesnake embossed in silver that he could hang around his neck from a silver chain. They made love before breakfast, the first time he had done so since his honeymoon.

Afterward she got him into the bathtub again and washed him as a loving mother might wash a child. Then she took him to a ranch outside Vegas where they rented horses and went riding. It was his first time on a horse and he nearly fell off but she rode expertly.

The cold early morning air, the beauty of the desert with the sun just beginning to rise gave him a new sense of the beauty of life. They made love in the sagebrush.

Back in the hotel he had to pack and catch the afternoon plane to New York and his final bankruptcy. He tried to give her some money but she refused

Like gambling, getting married in Las Vegas is easy, probably easier and cheaper than anyplace else in the States.

Chapel of the Bell

FLOWERS • PHOTOS
IMMEDIATE CEREMONIES
LUCKY
WEDDING
CHAPEL
OPEN 24 HRS.
GOWNS - RINGS
PORTRAITS.FLOWERS
CHAPEL & GIFT SHOP

to take it. He said he would only lose it at the tables on his way out. She urged him to try his luck one last time.

Well, he didn't win. He lost everything. But it didn't matter. The Nurse took him to the plane and waited until it took off. She gave him a farewell kiss and whispered that he was the greatest lover in the world and she would always remember him. He got on the plane and went back to New York and was never seen again. Sure he might have committed suicide anyway, but at least it wasn't in Vegas. And maybe that was his expected reward. Not much for his troubles, but better than nothing.

For this little job the Nurse received a hundred bucks from the hotel. But she felt as Florence Nightingale felt bandaging up wounded in the Crimea. Maybe she went too far, but she recognized a terminal case and gave her all. Maybe it didn't help the gambler but it helped her.

Not only her good works but her lack of greed made the Nurse famous. Yet as any moralist would have anticipated, she came to a bad end. She was perfectly happy combining her healing skills with her carnal needs and her desire for adventure, excitement, and change of scenery in the male anatomy. But one day there came to Vegas a Ravioli King. The Ravioli King was a man of fierce sensual appetites, the fire of which not even his degenerate gambling could quench. After having lost enough money to set him back in the manufacture of a million ravioli, he was introduced to the Nurse. He found her to be the girl of his dreams. He became madly infatuated. Not enough to leave his wife and children but enough for him to take pity on her. She was too good a person to be a hooker, no matter how high-class, so he felt. And he was not just a lover of honeyed words. When he told a girl he was crazy about her, he backed it up with cash. He convinced the Nurse to leave her life of sin. He opened up a boutique for her in Vegas with a guaranteed salary of five hundred bucks a week, tax free, under the table. But of course there were the usual lover conditions. She was to be faithful to him. (He would see her every two weeks for a period of four days.) And of course she must never again practice her healing profession in any sense.

The Nurse, madly in love herself, agreed to these conditions and for some months was happy with the arrangement. But life became too boring for her. She felt guilty about her comfortable no-risk existence. All around her in Vegas she saw the walking wounded of bust-out gamblers with no truly loving heart to console them. She felt like a slacker not taking a part in her country's war. But she was too much of a straight shooter to deceive the Ravioli King. She took to drink and then to drugs and finally she disappeared from Las Vegas.

THE BUSINESS LADY

But far more typical of the Vegas girl who trades sex for a living is Martha, also known as the Business Lady. She is a petite, demure young girl with a foxy pretty face and she approaches her trade in the great American tradition of engineering projects in depth. She is a top-notch technician in bed. She has a bookish conversation for the literary gamblers from the East. She has a movie patter for the filmmakers from Los Angeles. She has a girl specially trained by her when a customer requests "twins." The two of them go into erotic ecstasies over each other's bodies for the bon vivant voyeur who has paid handsomely for such stimulating tableaux.

Early on, the Business Lady made it a practice to develop lasting relationships with her customers so that they would call her whenever they come to Vegas. She ferreted out a top-notch accountant, a top-notch tax lawyer, a top-notch real estate man, and a first-rate gynecologist. She pretended to fall in love with them and refused to accept their money. What she took from them was their expertise. With that she bought a boutique to give her a legal source of income to justify her cash flow to Internal Revenue. That done, she could start buying up real estate and apartment houses. Her doctor friend from Los Angeles gave her thorough physicals and B-12 shots to

The national amateur boxing championship—the winners go to the Olympics.

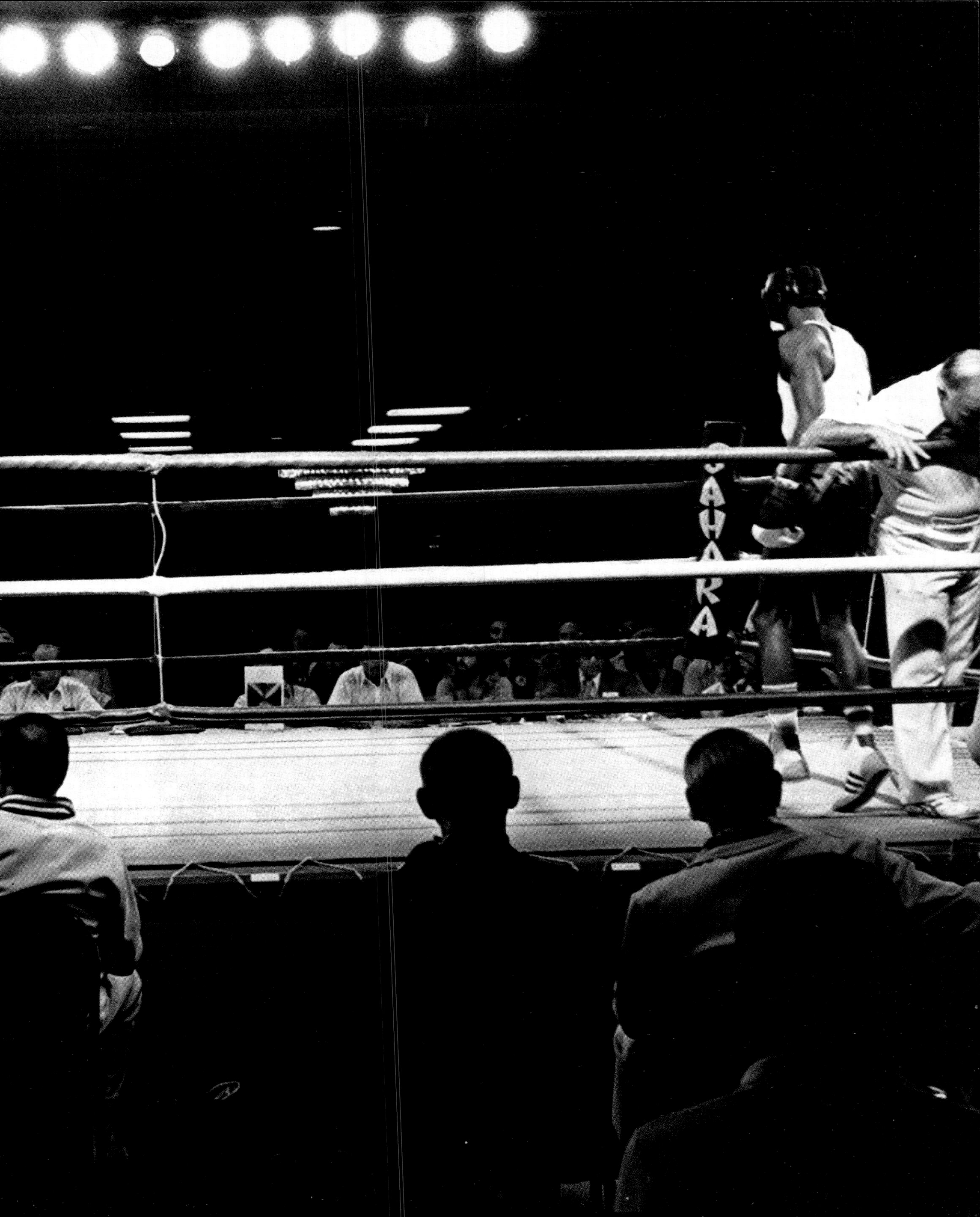

give her the maximum amount of working days.

She also fell in love with various Pit Bosses and hotel owners which was no big deal to them until she proved she could back up her falling in love with enormous expertise in bed, safety from venereal disease, and never asking for a favor unless it really was important. In short she completely manipulated the male world on its own terms until she became one of the wealthiest free-lance call girls in the history of Vegas.

She was actually a high-powered businesswoman. She delegated power like a business executive. She built up a string of girls to take care of her overflow and collected a commission from them. But as an agent, not a madam. She never gambled, never drank to excess, never smoked, never drugged, and, most important of all, she never really fell in love. She used her spare time to take liberal arts courses at the University of Las Vegas, not business courses. She dreams someday of writing a best-selling book about her adventures in Las Vegas and of returning to Malibu Beach, California, to get into producing movies. The affection and friendship she needs, as every human does, she gets from girlfriends she feels she can trust, never men. She is sober, industrious, and prudent in every way.

What can one say of a woman like this? That it is not a true success? Remember that she was a woman who felt she could not achieve in any other field. She did not have the proper skills, the right connections, the talent to acquire wealth in any other way. It can be argued that she was beautiful enough to marry a wealthy man but then she would in a sense have been his property, and to some degree, at his mercy. She did in fact often receive offers of marriage from wealthy men. She was never tempted. She does not hate men. She merely recognizes them as the enemy.

She leaves Vegas only to attend women's liberation activities around the country. She thinks sometimes of a political career. She claims that women's liberation must finally lead to the legalization of prostitution all over the world. But not as the vicious, idle, and stupid degradation it is now. Not as a woman's masochistic surrender to pimps or psychological self-destruction. No. She sees it as the economic clout women can use finally to achieve true equality with men. As a joke, maybe, she says, "Imagine a world in which you could meet a woman who has a Ph.D. in fucking."

THE MOST BEAUTIFUL SHOWGIRL IN LAS VEGAS

Of course she wasn't the most beautiful showgirl in Las Vegas. How can anybody make a judgment like that. Tastes vary. But she was a beauty. And she was typical and her life was typical of a lot of the showgirls who didn't get lucky.

She always caught the eye of the male stars playing Vegas. They would invite her to their suites to spend the weekend. Her stage manager had to give her the days off because of the magnitude of the star. So she would pack her bag and move into the suite. She would stay there while the star did his shows. She was his constant companion. They would make love, have dinner together, and she would hold his hand while he discussed power plays with his agent and his business manager and his lawyers. Sometimes it would be a female star, and she didn't mind. A star is a star.

For five years it was an exciting, pleasurable, and lucrative life. On Monday morning she would depart from the suite with at least five grand, maybe ten, in furs and jewelry and the assurance of the star if she ever needed a job. She was invited to all the parties of all the stars at all the hotels. But she was rarely outside of Vegas for a trip to New York or Europe. She sometimes went on a weekend to Malibu in California or the Beverly Hills Hotel. She was not particularly ambitious nor particularly talented. She was sometimes unhappy and sometimes in love with a musician or a straight fellow-dancer or the stage manager or director of her particular show. Life rolled on.

But she was like a millionaire living by dipping into capital. As she got older the beauty that was her capital diminished. She was still a very good-looking woman but no longer breathtakingly beautiful. She saw the stars no more, she worked weekends in her show if she was scheduled. There were some weekends with heavy gamblers from out of town but she wasn't really that kind of girl. And finally one day she was no longer beautiful enough for the shows.

The endings are various. They marry a real estate broker or a Dealer. (They sometimes do this at the height of their beauty.) They become Shills at the baccarat table. Some turn tricks for special handpicked customers. They spend their time fondly reminiscing about all the famous powerful men they have gone to bed with and tell stories about sexual peculiarities of those men who appear on TV to entertain millions of people. The juxtaposition of the star being folksy and bland on TV with a commentary on his sexual tastes amuses their friends.

For a few the reaction is that of a ruined millionaire in the Great Depression. They stick their heads in gas ovens, take killing pills, or drink themselves to death. I think some guy called it being "moths in a flame."

BEHIND THE SCENES

THE HOST

One of the important cogs in the casino operation, a cash-generating cog, is the Host. In the early days of Vegas, Jake Freedman, who started the famous Sands Hotel, gave small percentages to good Hosts.

A Host is an employee of the hotel. His job is to get gamblers from all over the world to come to his hotel. Once they come to the hotel his job is to make them happy in every way. Actually his job is to make them think they have died and gone to heaven.

The Host may live in Vegas or Houston, Texas, or New York City. The Host may be male or female. The female Host does not use her own bodily charms to make the client happy. Come to think of it neither does the male. She is all business charm. She is a buddy. She is usually a better buddy to the wife of the gambler than to the gambler himself.

In Vegas the Host will arrange for all show tickets, compliments of the house. He or she will arrange special dinners and parties, special luxury transportation for sightseeing and shopping trips. Credit for gambling at other casinos will be arranged. The Host is usually an excellent golfer willing to play for big stakes. A part of his income will be derived from this. He will also be an excellent gin player and some part of his income will derive from this. However, he will always arrange for this kind of gambling to be

These are really musicians.

done in foursomes so that he will not be the sole winner. That is, he will play golf and gin for high stakes with three gambler clients but it will never be head to head or everybody for himself. They will play two against two. The Host will always have a gambler-client as a partner against the partnership of two other gambler-clients. In that way he is not the lone winner stripping three clients. He is the buddy helping one client. Since his skills soon become known, he is traded around by the other three clients so that during the four-day spree he is at one time partners of each of them. He makes three buddies rather than three enemies. Then they also use him as a ringer with other friends at other hotels. This is not to say that this particular Host is a professional gambler or a pro golfer, he's merely an extremely skilled amateur. So skilled, in fact, that in golf he never beats an opponent by more than two strokes. He also sometimes loses. But he is the greatest eighteenth-hole golfer in the world.

Not all Hosts play this particular role. Many do not gamble or play any kind of games. But some Hosts come from a gambling and sports background so their skills are to be expected.

Hosts are always charming, affable, and have a special gift for comradeship. The Host will ask the casino to raise a client's credit limit so that he can gamble more money. He will bombard his clients with literature during the year about special events at the hotel such as backgammon and bridge tournaments. The Host will arrange special discounts at the hotel gift shops that deal in jewelry and furs and antiques. These shops have such a high markup that a 25 percent discount means nothing to them. The Host will also keep an eye open for unusual gifts to buy and give personally to top-notch gamblers.

Antique watches, antique jewelry, a gold money clip with a $100 chip in it. The cost is borne by the hotel but the gambler-client receives the gift as a personal mark of esteem from the Host who bestows it. A really powerful Host also may have "the Pencil," that is, he can sign all expenses at the hotel for the customer and arrange free shows and entertainment at any other hotel or restaurant on the Vegas Strip. So the Host also has to build a personal connection with casino executives all over the state of Nevada. Some Hosts even arrange for girls who are honest, healthy, and loving—no fears of VD or blackmail. The psychological theory that gambling drains sexuality or is a symbol of impotence may be true. But then what are those thousands of girls doing to those gambling men in the hotel rooms of Las Vegas?

And these are really cooks.

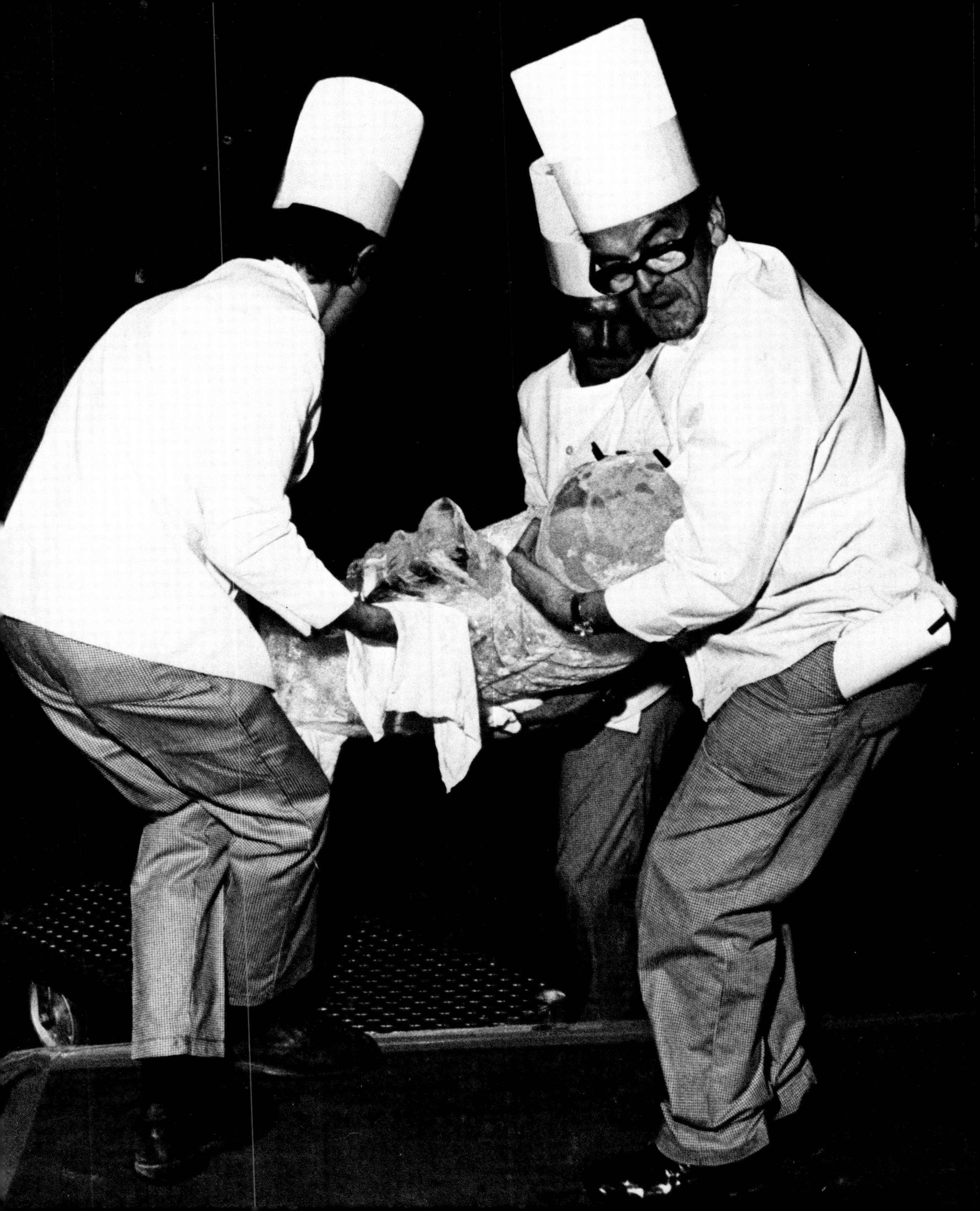

For outdoor types the Host arranges special expeditions to the Grand Canyon, horseback riding, the golf course.

Comps, the giving away of food, rooms, drink, girls, free airplane tickets, and show entertainment, started in Vegas in the 1940s. Actually it was part of gambling in England in the 1700s. In Vegas it began with cocktails, cigarettes, and cigars when some smart Casino Manager figured out the house lost money every time a player went to the bar for a drink. Hosts use comps wisely and generously.

Only a few Hosts have the awesome authority of "the Pencil" which authorizes a completely free stay in Vegas. The Pencil is strictly controlled. Only five or ten people in a hotel have it.

Hosts are used only at what are called "premium" hotels such as The Tropicana, Sands, Caesar's Palace, MGM Grand, and The Hilton. These are hotels that concentrate on big gamblers and not the blue-collar trade of Reno. There is also a difference between the premium hotels and some hotels on the Strip like the Sahara and the Fremont which cater more to conventions and package deals for their business volume. And then there are the Junket Masters who are partially hosts but have their own operation different and independent from the hotels.

THE JUNKET MASTER

First the definition of a Junket. It consists of a group of gamblers rounded up in a far-away city and herded on an airplane going to Vegas. The plane is chartered by the Junket Master. The group of people herded on the plane must have *money*. Usually they are solid members of society who earn a good living—garment center manufacturers, diamond merchants, doctors, lawyers, etc. In short they won't get hurt if they lose five or ten grand on a four-day spree in Vegas. They are not, for the most part, degenerate gamblers. They are social gamblers.

These gamblers get a lot of comps. The trip on the plane is free. The hotel room is free. The shows are free. Food and drink, within reason, are free. But unless they are rated at the top they have to pay for their own call girls, shows at other hotels, food in local restaurants. They do not get discounts at the gift shops. The Junket Masters, most of them, do not hustle girls, for reasons we shall see.

The social gamblers do not get all this without some commitment on their part. Some Junket Masters require that their clients put up anywhere from $2,000 to $5,000 in cash to go on the trip. When the clients check into the hotel they will receive this deposit money back, but in house gambling chips good only in that hotel. And they are expected to gamble. Never mind expected. If they don't they never get on another Junket. They don't have to lose. In fact if they win they will become more cherished by the Junket Master. They could also break even. But win, lose, or draw they must gamble, they must risk their money. Depending on the Junket, they should gamble at a certain level of stakes.

A guy on a Junket who sticks to one-dollar and five-dollar bets will not find space on the next Junket. He should bet $25 chips part of the time.

Wives and girlfriends are barred on most Junkets unless they pay their way. But many exceptions are made in this area. In recent years wives have even been included in the Junket on the theory that they could get the gambling bug. Also, instead of some strange pickup girl who will stash the cash, it will stay in the family to be lost on another trip. The drawback to this is that many men don't want their wives to know how heavily they gamble.

The Junket Master himself is usually a man who has an extensive background as a player or as a bookmaker or as a worker of some kind in illegal gambling establishments around the country. The concept of the Junket started in 1961 when a stockholder in a new big hotel flew in a bunch of his relatives and friends as a treat for the grand opening. Everything on the house. To the astonishment of the hospitable stockholder his planeload of friends dropped a big bundle of money, far exceeding the cost of the free trip. And so the Junket was born. Now most hotels have Junkets on a regular basis.

The Junket Master runs a complicated business. Let's take Harry Gold. Harry was a middle-aged bookmaker in the garment district in New York. The federal law requiring bookmakers to purchase federal stamps put him out of business. (The law was one of those Catch-22 things that put you in jail. If you complied with the federal law to buy stamps, then the state law got you for being a bookmaker. If you didn't buy the stamps, the feds jugged you.) Harry retired from the bookmaking business.

Harry organized his first Junket by contacting old customers and making them a deal. He chartered a prop plane because props were going out of service with the new jets coming in and so props were very cheap. Very slow too. But Harry made sure there was plenty of booze on the plane as well as some wild broads. (Every opening has to have something extra.) The hotel paid him $50 for every customer he checked in. The hotel picked up the tab for food and drink. The hotel followed Harry's recommendation on how much credit to give to each customer. There was a catch. If a

customer didn't pay his markers Harry was responsible. He collected or made good.

So Harry the Junket Man was very careful picking customers for a free ride to Vegas. Over the years he kept his own credit ratings. He weeded out the poor players who cut down his profits. He renegotiated his agreement with the hotel so that he would not have to make good unpaid markers. He would have only a moral obligation to see that they were paid. This is a lovely bit of phrasing. What is really meant was that Harry would only have to pay if he were terribly careless in the screening process. If the hotel made a good profit on his Junket, it would not press him to pay the bad markers of the trip.

Another rule that Harry made was that no client on his Junket was to get his credit limit raised without Harry's personal okay. This was one of his shrewdest moves. A client who went on a Junket with a credit limit of ten grand and lost his ten grand the first day usually begged and screamed for more credit. What could he do for the remaining three days in Vegas without gambling money? Harry was a stone wall. No more credit. He would play gin with the guy in his hotel room for a penny a point; he would take him golfing, even horseback riding. He would fix him with free shows or call girls, but no more gambling money.

Because Harry had found out the hard way that if he raised a client's credit

AGE
MINIAT

limit and the client lost another ten grand, he, Harry, would get the blame. The man had gone to Vegas budgeted to losing ten grand. Harry had enticed him on that plane and then deliberately set out to ruin him by giving him more credit. So the loser-client decided two things usually. He would never go on a Junket again. He would not pay his markers, not even the first ten grand he had planned to lose. Harry the Junket Master was left holding the bag filled with worthless markers. He lost a customer forever. He got a bad reputation. Because, of course, the welshing loser had to justify his position by bad-mouthing Harry all over town.

And yet if Harry gave the client more credit, and the client bailed out and won, he never was grateful to Harry for giving him the chance to bail out.

And then Harry found out another thing. When he refused to up the loser's credit the loser might get angry while they were in Vegas, but back home when the gambling fever had subsided, the loser inevitably thanked Harry and reserved space on the next Junket. And most important of all, the loser paid his markers.

So Harry adopted the rule. Never increase the credit limit granted to a player before he left home. It became Harry's proudest boast that he never let one of his players ruin himself. His reputation soared. Friends recommended new customers. Harry finally wound up running six junkets a year to Las Vegas, all of them profitable. His client files filled his office. He had thousands of names to call on to fill his chartered planes. It was gravy.

Of course there was a lot of hard work. He had to organize the Junket, charter the plane, make arrangements with the hotel. He had to use his judgment. Which players could bring their wives or girlfriends for a free ride? Sometimes a big gambler had a buddy who didn't gamble but wanted to make the trip to Vegas. Big is big. Harry gave the free loader a "ride" but he was never happy about it.

In Vegas Harry had to play the role of Host for his players and make sure they were happy. He also had to keep an eye on everybody and make sure everyone gambled enough to make the free ride worthwhile to him and the hotel. And he had to make sure none of his customers ruined themselves gambling.

After the Junket and fun are over, Harry has to keep after losers to pay their markers. In short, he is the pastor of the flock. It is a heavy responsibility and he feels he earns his money. But he is well rewarded. No Junket Master worth his salt earns less than a hundred grand a year.

But the most dangerous pitfall for a Junket Master is the infiltration of his

Junket by hustlers. One customer establishes himself as right guy. He introduces some friends who get invited on a Junket. Their IDs seem to be in order. They are recommended. These clients go on a last Junket, sign markers all over the place, and disappear with the cash.

Junkets had a great boom period but seem now to be in a decline. There are many reasons for this. In 1972 the Nevada Gaming Commission exerted direct control over independent Junket Masters. Las Vegas achieved greater and greater success with its program to bring conventions to the city. Some hotels bought or leased their own jets to bring customers in. Low-cost package deals became popular. And some hotels finally figured out that it might be cheaper to tell a big gambler to come on to Vegas whenever he felt like it and present his airline ticket for reimbursement by the casino. In effect the Junket Master who organized the customers had them stolen away from him as soon as their identities became known and their good credit established.

The Junket Master may be a dying species in Vegas because of a new attitude toward giving out free rooms and food and drink. Hotel owners think that Vegas is now such an attraction that people will come without the inducement of free room and board. Time will prove whether they are right. What is certain is that Vegas is becoming less and less of a bargain. Gamblers are no longer being wooed ardently. They are merely being politely courted.

THE COLLECTOR

This is a legend. A New York businessman went to Las Vegas and won a hundred grand. Naturally he didn't want the IRS boys to know about the win because he did not wish to pay the tax on it. (This is the gambler's Catch-22. If he loses he can't afford to pay his markers. If he wins he can't afford to pay the income tax on his winnings.) The casino offered him what was then a standard service. It would deliver the winnings by courier to him in New York. Arrangements were made. The money would be delivered to the Big Winner in the lobby of his New York bank on a certain day at a certain time. Then the big winner could pop the money right into his safe deposit box. The Casino Manager assured him that there was nothing to worry about. The Big Winner was given a receipt for his money. When the messenger delivered the cash the Big Winner returned the receipt. Which presumably the messenger then swallowed.

This was at one time a standard service in Vegas. So the Big Winner went back to New York. He worried a little about the messenger's getting mugged, but that was all. He went to

CLOSED
69
CLOSED
HI, I'm
FRED
From
WASHINGTON,
D.C.

the rendezvous at the appointed day and time and there waiting for him was the biggest toughest scariest individual he had ever seen in his life. This individual handed over the briefcase with the hundred grand and the Big Winner gave him the receipt. The Big Winner went to his safe deposit box and deposited the cash. It was all there, the full hundred grand.

Out of gratitude and also as a courtesy the Big Winner put in a long-distance call to the Casino Manager and told him he had received his money and voiced his appreciation. The Casino Manager said he was happy to oblige. The Big Winner assured the Casino Manager that he would be coming out soon for another shot at the tables and would surely stay at his hotel. The Casino Manager thanked him. The Big Winner said cautiously, "Jesus, that's the worst-looking guy I ever saw, your Messenger. A guy could get nightmares after seeing him." There was a silence on the other end of the line and then the Casino Manager said softly, "When you *lose* a hundred grand, that's the same guy we send to collect."

The point of the story of course is that Vegas can be very sweet to you as a winner and possibly very tough with you as a loser. Another point is that you win one day but you will almost certainly lose another day. To lose big you have to have a credit rating that is big. You must be able to sign a lot of

markers. But markers signed in the heat of gambling can get gamblers into a lot of trouble.

In short, the Big Loser cannot pay or will not pay. Such gambling debts are not legal debts by law in the state of Nevada. They are therefore not collectible in any other state. So casinos have to take their own steps.

Collectors for Las Vegas hotels generally no longer dare to use any kind of coercion to collect gambling debts. The hotels owned by conglomerates and big business corporations, officially, would not stand for it. Also Collectors are forbidden to try to collect from people who would be ruined by paying. Vegas does not want news stories or TV stories about how some wild-gambling redneck lost his 100-acre farm at the crap tables. But there are ways and ways. The following item is from the *Los Angeles Times* edited down.

A witness disguised in a ski mask told Congress Tuesday that some debt collection agencies used physical threats and cruel trickery to force payment of bills.

The mystery witness at a House hearing recounted anecdotes of his techniques, including the time he asked a woman by telephone what her shoe size was. When she responded he told her, "We're going to deliver you a pair of cement shoes your size."

Another time the witness said he drew a woman out of her home by impersonating a police officer and telephoning to say her son had lost both legs in an auto accident. The woman, in tears, walked into the trap at the hospital door.

"She thanked us that her son was still alive and paid the debt," he said.

Saying that he feared retaliation from former associates, the witness was disguised in a maroon ski mask, sunglasses, an aquamarine suit and tie and a glittering pinkie ring and using a pseudonym, "James Clark."

Clark said he had served as both an employee and a manager of collection agencies in a city he refused to identify.

He testified before a House Banking Subcommittee that is considering legislation that would bring the debt collection industry under federal regulation and provide fines and jail terms for illegal collection activities.

Clark said he collected debts ranging from large industrial accounts to record and book clubs whose bills sometimes did not qualify as legal debts.

Threats of violence were never carried out, he said.

Other pressure techniques, he said, included "beating" debtors psychologically by phoning them every five minutes through the day and telling terminally ill persons their heirs "would go through hell if they didn't pay us in full."

Note that this man was employed by high-class outfits like book clubs to collect their debts. Even reputable industrial firms and licensed finance companies used him. From my own experience I can relate a similar horror story. One of those house-to-house, apartment-to-apartment encyclopedia peddlers came around and sold me a two-hundred-buck set payable at ten bucks a month for ten years. As a bonus they sent a medical encyclopedia published in 1923. It wouldn't have helped my mother when she was raising me. Anyway I called and told them I wasn't paying. They said legally they had my wife's signature and I had to pay. I was living in a low-income housing project and making less than a hundred bucks a week. I needed every spare penny to gamble. I told them I'd see them in court. They tried a few phone calls and then a man knocked on my door and handed me a subpoena to appear in court. I looked at it carefully and saw that it was a printed summons but there was no signature on it. The County Court was nearby so I dropped around to see them. They told me the paper was a fake. I said I wanted these people prosecuted. I said I would testify against them and I gave the clerk all the information. He assured me the villains would be brought to book. I never heard from my creditor or the court again.

The point I want to make is that I never heard of Vegas Collectors acting so cruelly. Which is not to say that a Vegas Collector is an angel from heaven.

The Collector is a man hired by the hotel after the ordinary methods of collecting with admonishing letters have failed to make a debtor pay his markers. The Collector is usually given 50 percent of anything he collects. If the reneging debtor is a particularly hard nut he may get even more. But he is not allowed to make threats. However he can make scenes.

The Collector will pay a call at the debtor's business to make an arrangement. He will speak sweetly and reasonably. Why doesn't the man pay his just and honorable debt to the hotel that has hosted him so royally? After all, a debt of honor is sacred. If the man is strapped, monthly payments can be arranged. However, the Collector has with him two large and rather ugly gentlemen who listen impassively. This understandably makes the debtor nervous.

Now remember the Collector also understands gambling. He has been in the gambling industry himself in one form or another. He has been a bookmaker, a Shylock, a former Junket Master, or a Host. He knows the big law is not to send a gambler to ruin. If a debtor really cannot pay the Collector would never have accepted the assignment in the first place. So he knows the debtor can make some payment with a little pressure.

The Collector also knows that blue-collar workers earning up to fifteen grand a year nearly always pay their markers. He also knows that big gamblers who owe in the hundred thousands will pay their markers. Both these categories may just need a little friendly talk. The big trouble comes from those people who earn fifteen to fifty grand a year and these are usually professional people.

With these professional people the Collector makes two or three calls to their office. He will start a loud argument in a doctor's or lawyer's office or a small businessman's establishment. He will embarrass the man in front of his customers and clients and employees. He will be very loud, he will be abusive. He will be careful never to utter a threat. In effect he will approximate a divorced wife yelling for her back alimony. Surprisingly enough, this is an effective technique.

The Collector has other tricks up his sleeve. The gambler-debtor knows that gambling debts are uncollectible by law. But what the gambler doesn't know is that this is Nevada law. Puerto Rico law says that gambling debts made there are collectible. This means that if a gambler has markers in Puerto Rico he can be made to pay in New York. (You still can't collect a Nevada gambling debt in Puerto Rico.) When the Collector finds one of these he threatens to sue the man for the Puerto Rico markers if he

BLACK JACK PAYS 3 TO 2
Dealer

doesn't come to an agreement on the Vegas markers.

The Collector loves to call on automobile dealers, guys in speculative finance, real estate developers, doctors and dentists, housing contractors, road builders, Wall Street brokers, furniture store owners. He feels they are all crooks and knows they are susceptible to the vague menacing scenes he makes. His percentage of collections on these types is high. But the Collector sometimes comes a cropper.

Flushed with the success of his yelling and screaming and the presence of his two large chums, the Collector goes down to the New Jersey docks to collect from the foreman of a labor gang. The foreman is a hulking brute with muscles larger than a Texas oilman's bankroll. He looks down at the Collector contemptuously and says, "They sent *you* to collect off *me?* I'll throw you in the river."

The Collector then calls upon his almost forgotten reservoir of diplomacy. "What are you getting mad for?" he says sweetly. "I'm just asking."

Then he gets the hell out of there and sends the markers back to the hotel with the advice to forget the whole thing.

But the Collector knows how to deal with the crafty ones. There are gamblers who will give a casino a check for ten grand knowing that they only have eight grand in the account and the check will not be honored. The Collector takes this check and flies to the debtor's city. He deposits two grand in the debtor's account and then cashes the ten-grand check. This of course only when he knows there is no other way of collecting. How does he find out this crucial information? He bribes, cons, or romances a bank employee.

The Collector makes a good living and never gambles. He never hesitates to negotiate to get even 10¢ on the dollar and he's usually in secret sympathy with the debtor. But business is business.

He has only one worry. The Vegas hotels are learning that so-called legitimate collecting agencies will play far dirtier behind a facade of American business professionalism and will suffer less from bad publicity. After all, will the press make a fuss about a collection agency that works for General Motors and the giant finance companies or the large department stores? The Vegas Collectors, once so feared, may have become too soft and too vulnerable to do the job.

The Federal Gaming Commission reports that Nevada gaming is on the square. It has also discovered that Nevada citizens gamble more than tourists. Which proves that accessibility turns people into gamblers. It seems that there are three times more compulsive gamblers living in Nevada and that they gamble individually twice as much money as do people in other states.

My own inquiries indicate that the Nevada Gaming Commission has not received one complaint in the last four years about the collection of markers. It can reasonably be argued that some are too scared to complain. But the Nevada Gaming Commission guards the Vegas image fiercely and it did investigate one far-out case.

A famous movie producer in Japan organized Junkets to Vegas. The Japanese Junket Master was possibly responsible for the markers of his clients. One young man couldn't pay. Supposedly, threats were made. His mother, an old-style Japanese woman, kimona and all, complained to the police. The police swooped down and the Junket Master was arrested for extortion.

The Nevada Gaming Commission sent investigators over to see what was happening and the Japanese zeroed in and arrested them until things got straightened out.

What made the Japanese so tough was that Japan has a currency control law about taking yen out of the country.

Since the money was lost in Vegas but then collected in Japan, it became a little tricky. One Vegas hotel involved got its marker money back through

MORRIS

deposits in its account in Japan. The losers, in effect, were taking their money out of the country, against the law, simply by signing markers.

But this case also opened another question. Since gambling debts are illegal in Nevada, how can a hotel even put any kind of pressure on its debtors to make good their markers without being guilty of extortion? It's legally the same as a guy in the street asking you to hand over your wallet. On the first phone call you could prosecute and put the hotel out of business. Theoretically, some lawyers say, a class action suit could void all markers and the Vegas hotels would simply be out of luck.

The state of Nevada could make gambling debts legal. Then they would be collectible all over the United States. But the collection of such markers could ruin so many citizens that there would be a reaction against legalized gambling and federal or Nevada laws might pass, outlawing casinos, and Las Vegas would turn into dust.

And yet without credit gambling, without markers, the Las Vegas casinos could not exist. Because of some quirk in human nature (the fear of the word *welsher*) most people pay their gambling debts quicker than they do their medical bills.

THE VEGAS BUSINESSMEN

There are many ways to make your fortune in Las Vegas besides gambling. To own a gift shop in a plush Strip hotel is equivalent to having your own secret tunnel to Fort Knox. Gamblers on a winning streak have an irresistible impulse to buy hard goods, probably because they know they will lose the money back if they don't spend it.

The owner of a gift shop in one of the largest Vegas hotels supposedly paid $100,000 under the table cash for what is called "the key." This is in addition, of course, to the usual fees for the lease, the license, the rent, etc. The hundred grand was paid solely to be chosen as the lucky person to pay the exorbitant rent.

The gift shop owner was delighted. He stocked his store with items suitable as presents to women. He had mink coats, he had jewelry, he had all kinds of silver and gold ornaments; he had bracelets from India, chains from the Congo, elephant tusks from darkest Africa, complicated toys from Switzerland, all priced with a 500 percent markup. The gem of his collection was a locomotive and train built to scale, marvelously constructed, almost impossible to replace. He paid $1,000 for it as a showpiece and put it in the window. Not wishing to sell it since it was so effective, and knowing it would be difficult to replace, he put a price tag of $10,000 on it.

The very first day a man in a rumpled jumpsuit walked into the shop and said he wanted the locomotive in the window. The owner smiled and said, "It's too expensive." The man reached into his jumpsuit and extended a huge roll of $100 bills to the owner and said, "Take what it costs." The gift shop owner took his $10,000 and gave the man the locomotive.

A month later he managed to replace the locomotive. Again he put the $10,000 price tag on it. A huge fat Texan walked in accompanied by two leather-faced cronies. He also wanted the locomotive. The owner of the gift shop said, "Sir, do you know how much it costs?"

The Texan said, "I don't give a fuck what it costs, give me that locomotive."

The gift shop owner, a little dazed, then put in an order for three more locomotives which took him six months to get.

And so in Vegas the gift shop has anywhere from a 500 percent to 1000 percent "Edge" on the buyer which is a much better "Edge" than the casino has with its 1.4 percent in craps; its 5.86 percent in roulette; 10 percent in slots and 20 percent in keno and yet there are those who say that the gaming business is more avaricious than ordinary institutions of commerce.

One last comment on gift shops. There was a gambler called the Oklahoma Kid, a fabulously wealthy oilman who came every month to gamble away his oil depletion allowance, partially out of a sense of guilt that the tax laws gave him such an advantage. While he gambled he was as obnoxious as anyone could be. He pinched the cocktail waitresses and fought with the Croupier. He tried to cheat at roulette; he insulted the Pit Bosses. He started fights with his fellow gamblers. He was what the dealers of Las Vegas call a "Dr. Jekyll and Mr. Hyde," a familiar type of gambler. When he finished gambling, win or lose, he would go into the gift shop and buy a mink coat for the cocktail waitress, stake his fellow gamblers with a bankroll, send the Pit Bosses cases of champagne and boxes of Cuban cigars. The call girl went to his room to be presented with a diamond ring from the hotel gift shop.

To own a valet parking concession of a luxurious hotel is also to become rich. Again, such a concession, it is said, could cost you from 50 thousand to 100 thousand dollars under the table.

Then there are of course the men who make their living on women. Pimps find it very tough in Vegas. However, there are pimps and there are pimps. There are male charmers in Vegas who have love affairs with women and then sell their girlfriends to rich gamblers.

The word *pimp* is also a loaded word.

It is too pejorative in the same sense that one should not use the words *prostitute* or *call girl* or *whore*. It must be remembered that the great novelist Dostoyevsky borrowed money from women to gamble. The legendary Casanova performed his sexual acrobatics primarily to get grubstakes for the roulette wheel.

Julius Caesar, Claudius, Caligula, and Nero sold women slaves to pay off gambling debts.

In Vegas the technique goes something like this. The pimp will fall in love with a beautiful girl. She may be a visitor, she may be a showgirl. They have a very hot romance for a month. Then the lover comes to his woman with a tale of woe. He has lost all his money, he has signed markers. "They," the mysterious "they," will break his legs and cut off his nose. Only she can save him. He has a rich friend coming into town who is very shy with women. This rich man would give anything for the love and companionship of a beautiful woman. He will pay the markers, he will take them all to dinner. He is a great guy. Generous, witty, plays the saxophone and tap-dances almost like a professional. He is, it's true, a little old, a little fat. He is not as tall as one might wish and he does have a toupee and a bridge. But everything being equal, a true friend and a hell of a guy. It's up to her. Does she truly love him? She makes the great sacrifice. She gives her all for love and the pimp has killed two birds with one stone. He has made his score and has gotten rid of an encumbrance. He goes on to the next prospect.

However, this is not completely a sad story. Don't feel sorry for the girl. Most of them are pleasantly surprised that the man is not so terrible. He is perhaps not as witty, but he's nearly always as generous as her boyfriend has predicted, and if she gets real lucky, she may leave Vegas with an engagement ring and become the Lady of the Manor in Minneapolis or Providence.

Another way to make money in Vegas is to perform marriages. You open up a cute little chapel and become a member of the cloth and you get your chunk of the $24,000,000 that marriage and divorce generate in Nevada.

MORE GAMBLING TALES

There was a woman from Brooklyn. She lived a full life. She married and she had children. Her sons became successful professional men. Her daughters gave her grandchildren. Her husband operated one of the most successful delicatessens in Coney Island. She was a model hausfrau, a loving mother, and a faithful wife.

When she reached the age of sixty five her husband died. She knitted a great deal, she visited her grandchildren. Friends took her to Florida—Miami Beach. She found the people there too old. She visited a married daughter in California. She found the people there too young. On the way back to New York she stopped over in Las Vegas. And there she became a penny ante degenerate gambler, a not-so-rare species in America. She took a small apartment and settled down for a life of "sin."

In the South of France the penny ante degenerate gambler is a common phenomenon consisting of poverty-stricken nobility with complicated roulette systems, retired courtesans, English remittance men, American expatriates eking out their existence by fluctuating rates of exchange and their devotion to the spinning wheel.

In Vegas the Brooklyn lady gambled all day long. She read up on roulette systems. She played the slot machines until her shoulders ached. She accumulated treasure boxes full of nickels and dimes and quarters. She made friends with fellow penny ante degenerate gamblers and went for picnic lunches with them to Hoover Dam and the Grand Canyon. She never dipped into her savings. She used her Social Security and pension money to pay her rent and the rest she gambled on a daily budget.

It is not enough to say she was happy. She was in a state of bliss, entranced all day with the whirring slots of the casino, the red and black swirling numbers of the roulette wheel. The diamond-backed blackjack cards unfolding before her. She could forget her approaching death. She did this for fifteen years.

Her sons and daughters came to visit her twice a year. They brought her grandchildren to see her and receive presents from her. (She refused to leave Las Vegas for a single day.) But then, finally one of those old-age diseases began to grind her out like a casino percentage. She was bedridden and became frailer and frailer. But every day her cronies gathered around her bedside to play gin rummy and that is how she died, with a hand full of playing cards and an 87¢ loser on the sheet.

In the early days of Vegas an old desert rat collapsed outside a small-town casino. Good samaritans lifted him up, brought him into the casino, and laid him out on the blackjack

A million dollars in cash. Everybody can look at it—everybody can hope to win it. These are among the last one hundred $10,000 bills in circulation.

HORSESHOE
DOWNTOWN LAS VEGAS

table. A couple of degenerate gamblers gathered round and placed bets on whether he would survive until the doctor arrived. The "no" bettors would not allow any first-aid treatment because it would have interfered with the fairness of the bet.

This story, again like a lot of gambling stories, has a happy ending. The desert rat recovered. The "yes" bettors donated a portion of their winnings to give him a new grubstake when he left the hospital.

Perhaps the only foresighted, prudent degenerate gambler in Vegas history was named Odds Bodkin. He was a man of honor who always paid his debts. When he hit big he would make huge advance payments to a certain hotel, to three or four of the best restaurants in town, a clothing store, a jewelry store, his barber and his manicurist, and the madam of the nearest whorehouse so that no matter how badly the cards went against him he could live well without cash for the next few months.

Finally, in his old age his luck went bad. Two years of poverty broke his spirit. He couldn't believe that finally he was a loser and so at the age of seventy he sent letters to all his friends announcing that he was going to commit suicide. A devout Catholic, he asked his friends to intercede for him so that he would be buried in holy ground.

His friends rushed to see the local Catholic priest who indignantly refused their bribe offers. They went to collect their friend, who, they were overjoyed to find, on this final day of his life had finally gotten lucky. He had prepared the rope to hang himself and after doing so had reclined on his bed to recover his strength. While lying there he fell into a deep sleep and expired of heart failure. And so was buried in holy ground which assured him of his small percentage shot for Heaven.

At a classy Strip hotel the dice got really hot and action fast and furious. The lucky shooter became so excited stacking up $100 chips and throwing his winning dice that his false teeth fell out onto the green-felt table. The Boxman, without skipping a beat, whipped out his false teeth, and said, "You're faded!"

A hybrid degenerate Chinese-Swiss gambler named Gerhard Goda established a great and famous restaurant in San Francisco. For some years the Swiss blood predominated and he socked away huge amounts of cash since there is as much skimming done in restaurants as gambling casino counting rooms.

But slowly over the years his Chinese gambling blood boiled to the top and it became his custom to spend three or four days in Vegas every month. He was a desperado degenerate gambler and he lost huge amounts every trip, but the restaurant kept piling up the money.

The Vegas hotel began to feel a form of reverence not only for his celestial bad luck but his inexhaustible bankroll. Finally one day the hotel's owners decided to give him a birthday party. Four hundred Vegas gamblers were invited. As a climax a huge cake was wheeled into the dining room on shiny hubcapped wheels; the cake opened, the sides folded away, and there was a gleaming bright "Italian red" $30,000 Stutz-Bearcat automobile.

Gerhard Goda burst into tears at this sign of friendship, forgetting that his losses of just one year could have bought him at least ten of these magnificent automobiles.

The next year a rival hotel threw him a birthday party and presented him with an even more magnificent car, hoping of course to win his business away from the other casino. Again Goda burst into tears of happiness at finding such true friends.

This went on for six years. Gerhard soon owned a fleet of automobiles. Unfortunately his business died from neglect and the draining away of its life blood of cash. Goda closed the restaurant and came to Vegas. His friends drove the automobiles there for him. He proceeded to gamble away the automobiles. Gerhard became a penniless vagrant.

Again, as in most gambling stories, this has a happy ending. One of the hotels employed him as a Host and he performed his hosting functions magnificently. In the workshop garage of his home he constructs antique jewelry he gives away as gifts to his degenerate gambling clients who weep on his shoulder from the joy of his friendship.

In all the arguments about degenerate gamblers the discussion narrows down to what game holds the biggest fascination for the player—blackjack, shooting craps, roulette, baccarat, or the slot machines. The argument is finally resolved by this true story.

At the Sahara Hotel years ago, with the casino jammed with gamblers of all types, an anonymous threat came to the management that a bomb had been planted. The Casino Manager got on the loudspeaker system and announced, "A bomb threat has been received; please vacate the casino." Nobody moved. Five minutes later the Casino Manager announced again, "Please everybody leave the casino. A bomb threat has been received."

The blackjack players were the first to go, then the crap shooters (it could be that the dice were cold that night), then the baccarat players; finally the roulette players left. But the slot machines kept whirring and flashing. The players kept thrusting in their

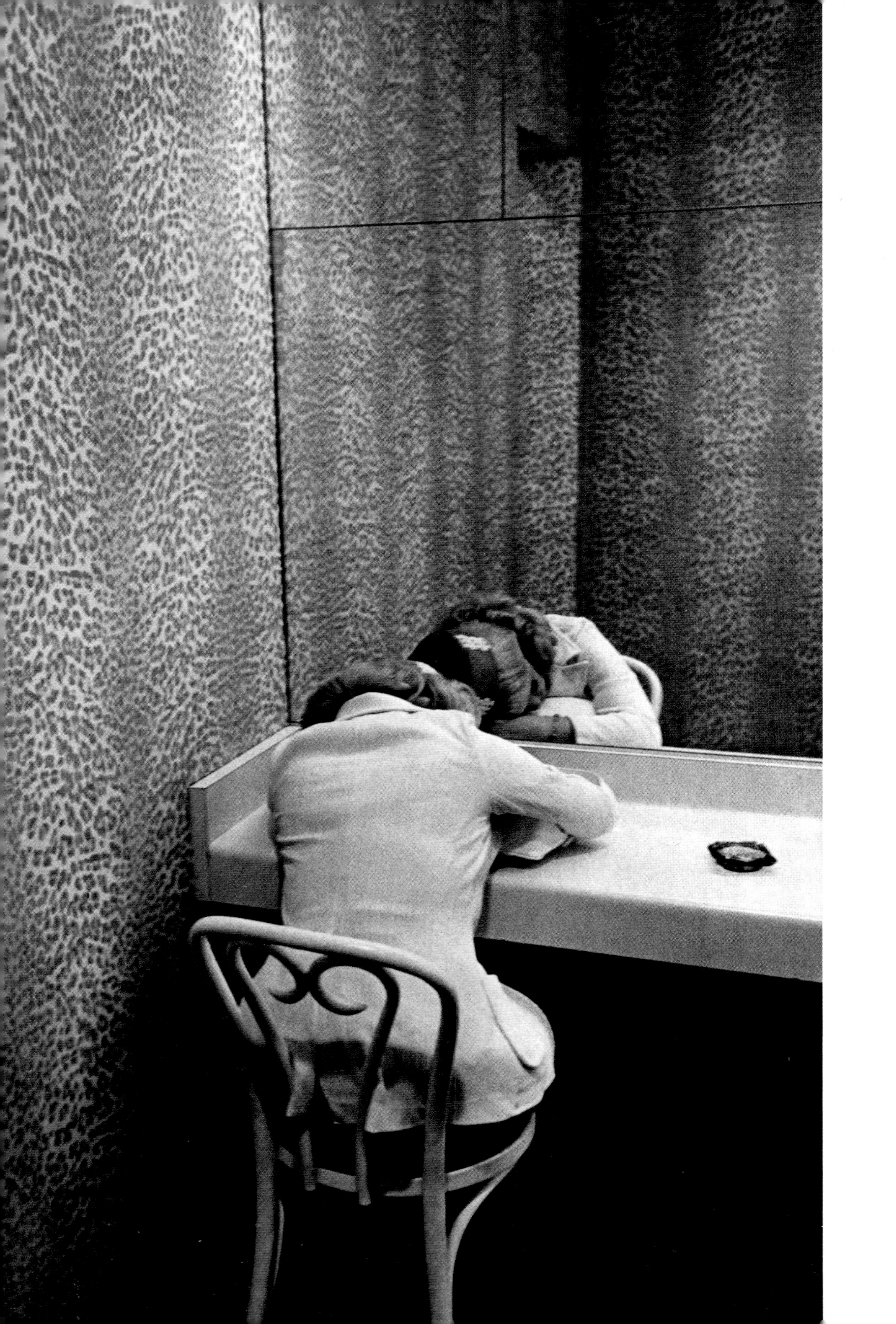

strangling grip that gambling had on mankind. We have other pleasures to relieve our anxieties, to divert our fears.

From my own experience I had to give up gambling at a certain period of my life because I found I could no longer write if I continued gambling. Now for the first time in my life, making more money than I have ever made in my life, more financially secure than I have ever been, I have come to the decision that I cannot afford, economically, to gamble. The simple reason being that to gamble is to risk, that is, to approach the "ruin factor." When I was poor the ruin factor was not important. Hell, I was ruined anyway. But now I have too much to lose and the "ruin factor" is decisive. Of course I had to lose a great deal of money and come near to "ruin" before I could figure this out. Gambling education is not cheap.

Everyone regrets his loss of childhood, even if it was an unhappy childhood, because then the world was pure and new. That is why so many people gamble. I think it is a desire to be happy in an innocent way. You can easily call this infantile. But I have noticed, as who has not, that the acquiring of knowledge does not necessarily make a man happy. The acquiring of power does not make a man happy. The acquiring of wealth does not always make a man happy. The love of a beautiful woman (throw in virtuous) does not invariably make a man happy. Certainly these all give him pleasure.

Saddest of all even being a "good" person does not make you happy. One of the most baffling enigmas is knowing men who have the serenity and happiness supposedly attainable only by Indian gurus and Tibetan monks and to find that, in these men at least, their celestial serenity springs from an unquenchable and unquestioning personal selfishness.

I think we are always searching for the happiness we had as children. And never mind about the many unhappy childhoods. I had what other people may call a terrible childhood but it was the only time I had moments of pure happiness. On a summer day getting up early in the morning to play baseball in the park without a worry in my head. Not a worry of any kind. It may be that as a kid you're pretty dumb. But I guess it's physical too. The response to the physical world is still so fresh. No signposts of trouble have yet been established in your mind. I guess maybe I'm talking about irresponsible happiness. And that's what gambling is to some degree.

And yet it is more than that. It is the gambling instinct in man that lifted him up the evolutionary scale, that has led to scientific progress. Why the hell should anyone want to get to the moon? Why should doctors inoculate themselves with diseases to test drugs? The motives are not entirely pure, based on humanitarian instincts. It is gambling.

We want miracles. When I was a kid and stole the Ace of Spades from the bottom of the deck, it was not only because it was a card that had extra value in our bets, but because it was a magical-looking card. Later when I gambled with my children and one of them was losing badly, I'd deal the Ace of Spades to him so that he could recoup a little. But that wasn't much fun. And then when I made a great success with a book I found that the pleasure wasn't pure, that I felt I had again dealt the Ace of Spades from the bottom of the deck.

Here is the terrible truth. I got more pure happiness winning twenty grand at the casino crap table than when I received a check for many times that amount as the result of honest hard work on my book.

Before anyone thinks I'm completely crazy let me say that I recognize that it was better for me as a social human being to earn my money by hard work. I realized that gambling could only lead to the ruin factor in my life. I was smart enough to give up high-stakes gambling before I went broke. Still the mysterious fact remains: Why did I so much more love getting and winning money in a way in which I had no control rather than in a way that was to my credit, supposedly?

I think, I think, that the whole magic power of gambling lies in its essential purity from endeavor, in its absence of guilt. No matter what our character, no matter what our behavior, no matter if we are ugly, unkind, murderers, saints, guilty sinners, foolish, or wise, *we can get lucky*.

And so I think gambling will grow and grow. There will be more Las Vegas cities, more and more casino gambling and lotteries and other schemes to take the people's money. But I don't think the gambling fever will be as dangerous to individuals. Remember again, that prior to the twentieth century there was very little to do in the form of amusement. There were no movies, no TV, very few people could read and there weren't that many books to read. Those guys who studied the Torah and the Bible didn't have much choice. Sure you could go hunting and go to wars and sail over oceans and there was always sex, but not much more. When playing cards were discovered it was no wonder that gambling became an epidemic and people went to the gallows for stealing money. And stealing not to feed their starving children, but to rush to the gaming tables. Today we have so many diversions, including drugs, that gambling is not a serious danger.

At least not to the individual. It is far more dangerous to our society as a whole. There is no question in my mind that widespread legal gambling decays the social structure.

Speaking for myself, I would rather be a degenerate gambler than watch TV. I look upon drugs with horror—but who is to say that in future years, when the dangers of drugs become more controllable, that they will not be as acceptable as gambling is today? But right now I would much rather my kids become gamblers than drug addicts or, what the hell, admit it, I'd rather they became degenerate gamblers than TV addicts. TV advertising is one of the most mortal insults to the spirit of man.

Right now, finally, I have "aged out" as dope addicts are said to do. I no longer really enjoy gambling, but the infantile lust can return. When I am too old for sex, when age withers my appetite for pizza and Peking duck, when my paranoia reaches the point that no human being arouses my trust or love, when my mind dries up so that I will no longer be interested in reading books, I will settle in Las Vegas. I will watch the ivory roulette ball spin, place my tiny bets on red and black numbers and some sort of magic will return again. I will throw the square red dice and hold my breath as they roll and roll along the green felt. I will sit down at the blackjack table and baccarat and wait for my own magical Ace of Spades to appear and I will be a lucky child again.

Should I go to heaven, give me no haloed angels riding snow-white clouds, no, not even the sultry houris of the Moslems. Give me rather a vaulting red-walled casino with bright lights, bring on horned devils as dealers. Let there be a Pit Boss in the Sky who will give me unlimited credit. And if there is a merciful God in our Universe he will decree that the Player have for *all* eternity, an Edge against the House.

FIRST
FROM ITALY
CITY
HAZARI
NEVADA'S
Alice

ARC
Entrance
entrance
Oriental
NEVADA
CLUB

A NOTE FROM THE AUTHOR

My thanks to Lanetta Wahlgren, Pam Kromer, Saundra Feingold, and Diane Belmonte for their research.

To Milton Stone and Alan Lee for instructing me in the folklore of Las Vegas.

To Anthony Puzo for his help in organizing the material, reading, and suggestions.

To Bob Markel, for THE idea, and his staff for its execution.

And, of course, most of all to the photographers John Launois and Michael Abramson.

A NOTE FROM THE PHOTOGRAPHERS

Las Vegas is a "private" town. NO CAMERA PERMITTED signs are prominently displayed at every hotel and casino in Las Vegas. Despite the legality of gambling in Nevada, this policy is designed to protect the anonymity of the guests.

For the photojournalist in this visual age when the media often make the event, and the photographer's concern is the reflection of reality, such restrictions posed a special challenge. The people in this book are real people, photographed in a documentary style, but never over their objections.

It is often said that "time does not exist" in Las Vegas. For us a total of fourteen weeks of time and energy would have come to naught without the gracious and unselfish cooperation of the people subsequently acknowledged:

- Don Payne, head of the Las Vegas News Bureau, and his dedicated staff, particularly Don English, who labored tirelessly to assist in every possible way.
- Alan Lee and the Tropicana Hotel for their gracious hospitality and assistance.
- Kirk Payne, for his special assistance to John Launois in the production of the color photographs.
- Jim Brann, head of public relations at the Union Plaza Hotel, who constantly opened the doors for us to photograph his casino.
- Michael Gaughan, co-owner of the Royal Inn Casino.
- Jack and Benny Binion, the father-and-son owners of the Horseshoe Club.
- Terry Lindberg, former director of public relations at the Stardust Hotel, for allowing us to photograph backstage at the Lido de Paris show.
- Tex, Tracy, Tiffany, and Michelle for allowing us to photograph backstage at the Cabaret Burlesque Club.
- Jeanne MacGowan, public relations director of the Dunes Hotel.
- The bellhops, dealers, waitresses, gamblers, security men, cocktail waitresses, and the friendly strangers from all parts of the world who treated us to many kindnesses and hospitalities.
- Lastly, Howard Chapnick of Black Star, whose insight into Las Vegas and whose photographic guidance were invaluable. His involvement did not end until he did the preliminary editing of over 15,000 images which provided the raw material for this essay.

John Launois, Michael Abramson, and Susan Fowler-Gallagher